TWELVE MAD MEN

A NOVEL OF STORIES

BY

VARIOUS ARTISTS

CURATED BY RYAN BRACHA

Contents

Introduction

Twelve weeks ago, I approached some writer friends about an idea I'd had. All I knew is that it featured a lunatic asylum, twelve residents, and one narrator, and would be written according to some set rules or guidelines. I stole the idea of the rules from the Dogme 95 film movement that appeared in the mid-nineties from the Scandinavian film industry, spearheaded by Lars Von Trier, and then to a lesser extent, Harmony Korine who tried to bring it to an English speaking audience. I had no clue as to the plot, or the narrative at all. I just knew I wanted to give it a go. I'm nothing if not ambitious with my writing. I don't like 'safe', I don't think it does an artist any good to write the same old tripe that's churned out by Tesco bookshelf writers in less than the time it takes you to actually do your big shop there. Don't get me wrong, they've found something that works for them, and they are writing, so fair play and more power to them for doing it. But it's not how I roll. I want to be remembered by the few people that will remember my writing, as being somebody who liked to challenge himself.

So I approached these eleven supremely talented gentlemen, and I asked them if they'd like to 'play' themselves in the book. To tell the stories of how these fiction versions of them came to be in this lunatic asylum. They could be as violent, sweary, funny, or filthy as they wanted to be, and all they had to do was tell the story of how they got there. I would do the rest, in that I would weave these stories into the narrative, improvising and reacting to the content of these eleven tales, or twelve if you included the final one, which I would write. I didn't expect anybody to get involved. I thought they'd tell me I was being an idiot, but they didn't. Everybody I asked straight away accepted the invitation. Except one, a huge traditionally published name who I thought I'd take a punt on asking. He was too busy, and shall remain nameless, and I think the book is probably better off without his involvement. Instead, it gives this phenomenally talented group of indie writers a chance to showcase their most depraved sides, in an unusual and innovative novel which I would hope will strike some chords. I hope that readers get a kick out of the way the whole affair has been laid out for them. I hope that writers see that we have this huge and useful tool available to us nowadays that means we can be as daring, and challenging as we like, as long as we tell a great story. And I hope that when all is said and done, you enjoy this work, as much as I enjoyed putting it together. Ladies and gentlemen, please be upstanding, and welcome some of the finest writers I've ever had the pleasure of working with. Paul Brazill, Gerard Brennan, Les Edgerton, Craig Furchtenicht, Richard Godwin, Allen Miles, Keith Nixon, Darren Sant, Gareth Spark, Martin Stanley, and Mark Wilson. Go and look their works up, you won't be sorry that you did.

Ryan Bracha – July 2014

I'm the porter
and these halls I walk
from wall to wall
are full of the types of minds
that might sometimes
fight the binds
of thought paths that we all default to

- *Porter,*
Dan Le Sac Vs Scroobius Pip

Lyrics used with the kind permission of Scroobius
Pip.

12 Mad Men

We're all here for a reason.
I don't know how I got here. That much is true. The why is another thing altogether. I know that, now. I'm here for a reason. I'm the same as Miles and Edgerton. I might have once thought it but the truth is that I'm no better in the head than Brennan, Spark, or that crazy fuck Wilson. As much as I would love to, I can't say I deserve to be here any less than Nixon, or even the mad yank Furchtenicht. I'm on a par with Brazill, level pegging with Stanley, going toe to toe in the fucked up mentally unstable rat race with Godwin. Hell, it's a stalemate between Sant and me. We're all the same. We all have our stories, and our foibles. Our bug bears. We all have our coping mechanisms, some a little further off the tracks than others. We all have a favourite colour. A favourite member of staff. A favourite drug. A favourite method of receiving torture for the purposes of science. I'll repeat myself in case you already forgot; I don't know how I got here. I do know why, now. We are definitely all here for a reason. There's no shame in it. That's what they tell you. That's what they tell all of us, the twelve men that live here at St. David's, or St. David's asylum for the criminally insane, to give it its proper title. Us, the twelve mad men.

One

The bulky bastard approaches me. He looks well built, but there are the perky big mouse's noses of slowing forming bitch tits underneath where there maybe used to be pecs. You can see it beneath the uniform. These tits enjoy a glorious view of his mountainous gut which hangs just over the too-tight trousers that stretch like a drum skin over his prominent cock. It's not the first thing I noticed, but you can't help but see it. He stands about my height but like I say, he's a big cunt. His ruffled brownish hair doesn't look it's ever seen a brush, and there are sparks of grey around the temples. Ginger sideburns crawl down his round face then curl up and die in uneven levels beneath his ears. Aside from that I'd say he wasn't a bad looking bloke, if that kind of bloke was your thing. His smile reaches his eyes as he greets me warmly, shaking my hand. Firm, but not hard. Soft, but not womanlike. I return his greeting, forcing my eyes away from that bulge in his trousers.

"Nice to meet you," he says, genuinely seeming to mean it.

"You too," I say neutrally. It's my first day, he could turn out to be an utter prick, but in all honesty first impressions are boding reasonably well, so I afford him a thin smile.

"You got your uniform then, eh?" he asks, noting my attire. *Yes, I got it, I'm wearing it,* I don't say.

"Yeah, nice one," I say, and find myself looking down at it, as if it's the first time I've laid eyes on it, before I cough self-consciously, "is there anywhere I can put my bag?"

He nods, and turns on his heels, heading away from me.

"Yeah, come on, I'll show you. I'm Benny, by the way."

I follow as he meanders down the hallway and pauses by a door, looking for me to speed up my pace, which I do. He swipes his card and enters the room, holding the door for me.

The staff room is dark, in the poorly lit sense. A bulb in the corner buzzes monotonously, obviously only a few breaths from certain death, and somebody just hasn't had the heart to put it out to pasture, like an aged dog, wheezing its way to the light at the end of the tunnel in its own sweet time. Fuck what anybody else wants out of the situation. I'll get there when I'm ready. It's not long before the buzz of the bulb fades into normality. As I drop my bag into the locker that Benny, my new colleague, has assigned to me, a wail of anguish comes from somewhere else in the building. Like somebody opened a rusted iron door amidst the sound of somebody else boiling a hundred lobsters. I'm not totally convinced that it was a human sound, but my colleague catches my look of concern and smiles.

"That'll be Keith," he says nonchalantly, "he does that."

We wander the corridor, him talking and me looking at the state of the structure. As he tells me that St. David's was built in eighteen sixty something I'm seeing water drip from a dark brown spatter on the ceiling into a half full blue bucket, a decreasing circle of dried splash stains around its base. When he says that it was built by a man called Benedict something I'm distracted by a speckled patch of moulded damp which reaches up from the dusty skirting to the light switch in the middle of the long grey wall. As he tells me the name of the head doctor, or psychiatrist or whatever they call them here my eyes are drawn to the brown sign which points whoever to wherever. Something to do with some sort treatment. I'm not being awkward with my descriptions here, I promise. It's just that sometimes when you're in a new place you don't tend to pick up the details. You only see the big things. Maybe if and when I've been here a bit longer I'll notice the details. Maybe. I can't promise anything though. Don't hold your breath. Really, please don't.

"We have twelve residents at present," he says, "we call them that," he says, "not inmates."

Parts of the tile flooring have come away and it's just that ridged concrete you get underfoot. A trip hazard if ever I saw one.

"Some have been here longer than others, some crazier than most, you know what I mean?"

Flies skitter around a dark patch on the floor. Health and safety would have a field day. I wonder when they last had an audit.

"They use some unorthodox methods, but these fellas' heads aren't gonna get any better by themselves, so, y'know, no harm in trying, eh?"

Doors pass us by, each with a different method etched into the scratched black name plates. *Bleeding therapy, intimidation therapy, electrical therapy, medicinal therapy, hypno-regression therapy, alternate therapy.* Seriously, the list goes on. As Benny says that one of the doctors here, a somebody something, practically invented one of the therapies I'm side-tracked by areas around the doorframes at shoulder height, where the paint on both sides has been scratched away in long deep ridges. I think that a decorator would be a wise investment. Or a demolition crew.

From somewhere above us, that howl comes again, echoing from every stained wall and surface around us, increasing the volume tenfold. A shiver twitches at the base of my spine and then shoots directly up, like a bungee rocket on the fun-filled coast of some Balearic island, into the crook of my neck.

"Shut the fuck up, Keith," Benny says in a bored tone, and turns to me, "that's Keith again."

The lights flicker intermittently and he sighs.

"Seriously, man, they could really do with an electrician around here."

I silently concur with that opinion, and offer a slight smile.

"You sure you don't have any questions?" he asks as he stops sharply, I shake my head, no. He shrugs.

"Okay, well, you know, just ask if you do, they say there's no such thing as a stupid question. Hey, what you reckon the first sign of madness is?"

I shrug.

"Suggs coming up yer driveway!"

I don't get it, but he's overcome with the apparent hilarity of it for a good ten seconds. This booming laugh spewing from his chest. I say nothing.

The ascent to the first floor is silence, punctuated by the percussion of the claps of mine and Benny's shoes against the hard cold floor, and the gentle wheeze from his lungs that gets heavier with each step we take. Benny turns to me at the top and smiles.

"I really ought to get back into shape, I used to be a champion boxer, you know?"

"Really?" I ask, genuinely intrigued, but not enough to dig further than that. He nods. Takes another breath.

"Yeah, amateur champion for my county for two years straight," he says, then shakes his head in regret, "now I'm just a fat smoker."

I laugh politely through my nose at his self-deprecating humour, but the truth of it is that I've never been one for self-deprecation. It's a cry for somebody to object. To tell you that *no, you aren't that fat*, or *really, you're beautiful, stop putting yourself down*, or worse, *no, you're a really good writer/singer/painter*, delete as appropriate. You really are that fat, you look like a bulldog licking the piss off a nettle, and your poetry makes the hairs go up on the back of my neck because I'm literally embarrassed that you chose to spout your shit in public. Harsh? I don't think so.

"That's cool," I say.

He seems happy with my response and moves on, opening the doors to the first floor.

"Now this," he says, "is where the real fun is."

The lights seem brighter up here, but no less sporadic in their ability to achieve sustained periods of doing what they're supposed to. Before us there are eight doors. Four along one wall, four along the other. At the end of the corridor there's a large window of about eight panels. Beyond that is pitch black nothing.

"Okay, so up here we've got Wilson, he's Scottish," he says with a pointed look on his face that says I should know what he's implying, but I really don't, "and Miles, or *Melluish*, he calls himself that. There's Furchtenicht, he blinded one of the counsellors with a paint brush. Then there's God-"

He doesn't finish the sentence, because the lights fizz harshly, like somebody with an electro larynx having a fit, and shut down. In the glum of the emergency lighting Benny's head drops. He sighs.

"Fucking hell," he says, "not ideal at all," he says, "I probably should have mentioned this first."

As if on cue there are fists hammering against doors. Voices all meld into one desperate plea for help. The voices echo hard against the walls and into my skull.

[13]

"Look, I shouldn't ask you to do this, it being your first day and all," says Benny, "there's training that you need to do usually, but we're in a bit of a bind." Nobody mentioned training before. The thumps and chanting make my eardrums vibrate.

"See, there are processes we need to follow in the event of a power outage," says Benny, "to ensure the comfort of the inmates," he says, "I mean residents." The sounds hurt my head. The only thing I can compare it to is an adult version of a children's play area in some chain pub, the ball pool and the slide and the climbing frame. You can try to think, but it's impossible. He slides a bunch of keys into my hand quicker than the time it takes for me to realise I'm holding them. He looks into my eyes, a seriousness, and a focus that until now had been lacking from his demeanour.

"I need you to help me to calm them down," says Benny, "they won't hurt you, they know better." This cacophonous noise threatens to derail me. I thought this was supposed to be a simple night guard role, with a comfortable chair and a crossword. So far all I've had are Victorian structures with Victorian methods and the howls of some maniac called Keith. I don't like it. He registers the discomfort than swipes across my face like the wipe-clean mechanism of a *Magnadoodle.*

"Look, you just knock on the door," says Benny, "and as you go in you say 'Get in the corner, I'm here to fix the lights' and that's it. They know the drill. They'll get in the corner. Seriously, they'll sit there for hours after that."

He must then register the newly formed doubtful look on my face because his hands come up, open palmed.

"Really, just do me that favour, I need to go and fuck with the electrics and call it in, or they'll be at it all night. Once, that happened, it's not much fun, I can tell you."

I don't get a chance to decline the request, or voice any concerns because Benny is away. His fat, former boxing champion arse shuffling through the door and down the stairs as fast as his legs will take him, leaving me to myself in the empty corridor with the tormented yowls of insane men. It's at this point that I consider heading back downstairs myself, grabbing my bag and disappearing from St. David's for good, but I don't. I don't know why. Instead I focus on the first room on my right. The door visibly shakes as the maniac behind it smashes against it for his life. I don't know how I got here but already I'm in front of the door. My hand finds its way upright, and I knock on the metal. Beside the door is a rectangle of slate. Upon that rectangle is a name. It reads *Brazill, Paul D.* From the other side of the metal is a harsh thump. A scraping hush. A voice.

"I can smell you," it says. I hear an odd mix of accents. Not exactly from this country, but not *not,* if you know what I mean. A purr, "you aren't him."

"Get in the corner, I'm here to fix the lights," I say, almost robotically.

"Where is he?" the voice asks.

"Get," I say, stuttering as a weak involuntary gasp breaks my speech, "in the corner."

"Did he die?"

"I'm here to fix the lights."

"Did you save me his heart?"

I push the key into the lock, only, my hand won't twist. I slam my hand against the metal, hard.

"Get in the corner," I say, as calmly as I can.

"You smell," says the voice, "delicious."

[15]

"I'm here to fix the lights," I say.

A moment of quiet follows. Then the voice.

"Fix away."

It seems more distant. Maybe Benny was right. My right eye twitches. My breathing becomes harsher. My hand twists the key. I really shouldn't be doing this. Surely there should be a risk assessment completed before this. The lock clicks. Am I even insured? My hands work independently of my will, and the handle is pressed down. A buoy of nausea bobs uneasily in my throat, a flashing beacon warning me from my next action, but I can't help myself. The door swings open, casting a dull glow into the darkest shade of black I've ever known. The black spills into my vision like the stinking pus from a lanced abscess. Almost from nowhere and in excess. The room that holds the darkness hostage can't be much more than six or seven feet both ways, and that dull glow of the emergency lighting slowly dilutes the black, to reveal him. He's standing in the corner, like Benny said he would. His fingers dance by his side like he's performing some paroxysmal shadow puppet act against the dismal light, and my eyes drift up from the redundant show to his face, with its high forehead and twitching cheeks which crease up as he smiles at me.

"I'm no trouble," he says, his accent now definitely northern English without the blunting force of the metal door and my fear of the unknown, "I'm no trouble at all."

I say nothing.

"You smell good," he says, "really good," he says, "do you want to hear a story?"

A Man Of Sophisticated Tastes

by Paul D. Brazill

IT ALL STARTED on a sleepy
Sunday night in Astros Wine Bar. Last orders
hung over us like a middle-aged spread and
the conversation was as weak and strained as
my gran's tea. I could feel the cowl of sleep
smothering me.

'It's not prejudiced,' said a well-sozzled Len
Lien, becoming uncharacteristically animated.
'I've just never met a Welshman I didn't want
to twat. The Jocks and Micks and fine. But the
Welsh all seem to be whingers. Always
bleatin' like sheep.'

'Must be genetic,' I said.

'I met a Welsh cannibal once,' said Neil Lien.
'She was alright. Fit as a butcher's dog, like.'

I sneaked a peek towards the bar. Patsy, the
pasty faced barmaid, was giving us the evil
eye. She was desperate to lock up so she
could get home for a bit of nooky, what with
her Raymond being back from the oil rigs for
the first time in months. She was gagging for
it, apparently.

Patsy put on a Lloyd Cole CD, knowing that it
was as likely as not to clear us out of the place
although I actually quite liked him. Not that
I'd have admitted that to the lads.

We'd been in the same band for nigh on ten
years and although one of the reasons we'd
spilt up was because we weren't making the
dosh, musical differences was certainly

another one. It was like so many relationships, I suppose. We just grew apart. Well, I grew and they didn't.

The rest of the band were more than content to plod along knocking out the usual bog standard blues rock but me, well, I'd always had more sophisticated tastes and had wanted to broaden our musical horizons.

'Oy, aye,' said Len. He yawned and farted. 'An actual cannibal?'

Len was like Fun House mirror version of Neil. Or maybe it was the other way around. Both were tall, bald and with thick framed and lensed glasses but whereas Neil was skinny as a rake, his brother was built like a brick shithouse. They'd been a tight arse rhythm section once upon a time though.

'Well, just had a quick nod and hello with her, like,' said Neil. 'She was with John Turnball. Saw them together doing the tonsil tennis one night when we were down the Indoor Bowls Club.'

'Who the fuck's John Turnball,' I said.

I wiped my glasses with a paisley, silk tie I'd picked up from the Scope shop the day before. Shuffled around a bit in my seat. I was sinking into a battered old leather armchair, sucking on the ice cubes from my drained white wine and soda. I'd been taking my time with my drink. Not because I didn't want to get hammered – I always wanted to get hammered - but because I was strapped for cash.

'You know, John. Course you do. Lives above that burnt out kebab shop, over King Oswy Way. Got that Tourette's,' said Neil.

'Oh, you mean Fuck-Off John. Why didn't you say so? Well, he's a right head the ball,' I said. 'I certainly wouldn't believe anything he says. He's a walking chemists shop for a start. Scrambled eggs for a brain.'

I shuffled my arse to get rid of the numbness. 'Did she have a bone through her nose an' that,' said Len. Face beaming like a door stepping Jehovah's Witness.

'Who Fuck-Off John?' said Neil.

'Naw, yer daft twat. The cannibal,' said Len.

'Told you, she was well tidy. Blonde bit, early twenties. Nips like organ stops,' said Neil. 'All suntan, sunglasses and leather trousers so tight you could read her lips.'

'She could eat me anytime, then,' said Len, and we all forced a laugh.

Patsy rang the last orders bell and the subject quickly changed to the more pressing matter of who was getting the last round in. As per usual, Neil bought the drinks. He was the only one of us with a regular income – he played drums in a U2 tribute band called Me Anall - and I was particularly brassic, what with me losing my job at the council and owing my landlord Herbert Walker a wad load of back rent.

'Best knock these back sharpish,' said Neil, putting down the drinks on the sticky table. 'Or Patsy'll bar us out again.'

'Wouldn't be the end of the world,' I said. 'There's more to life than Astros, you know? There's a big wide world out there.'

'True, true,' said Neil. 'There's a new Wetherspoon's opening up just off York Road next week. And they do cashback. He grinned

[19]

and patted his jacket pocket where he kept a fistful of hooky credit and debit cards he'd obtained.

'Yeah, but I hate those places,' said Len. 'Full of lowlifes.'

'True,' I said. 'Wouldn't do to let our standards slip.'

***

In the early hours of the morning, as my hangover kicked me into an unwelcome consciousness, I had a moment of inspiration. Lying in my sweat soaked bed, I could feel cogs and wheels whirring in my brain, as well as my guts. I stayed awake all night working on a perfect plan and when it got to a relatively civilised time, took my Nokia off the bedside table and phoned Fuck-Off John. The phone rang for ages and then he answered.

'Arsewipe,' he said.

'Alright John,' I said and told him who I was.

'Who the fuckin fuck?' he said.

'You know? Brian's brother.'

After about five minutes of verbal abuse about nuts and coffee, I managed to arrange a meeting with him in the pub for a lunchtime session.

I called in at my brother's to cadge some dosh from him, since he was always flush. A lot of builders had lost work due to the Poles doing the work cheaper, if not better, but not Brian. I got to Astros Bar just after 11.30 and John turned up not long after. We got our drinks and stood at the bar for a moment.

'Patsy not working today?' I said to Simon, a camp wock-eyed Irishman in his late forties.
'Oh, no. She's on a promise, she is. She'll be bandy legged for a month.'
We looked around the room. A crumbling pub with a crumbling clientele.
Fuck-Off John nodded toward the fire exit and I followed him.
'What's the story with the maneater, then?' I said.
'I fuckin met the cunt online, like,' said John. He popped a tablet the size of a Trebor mint and washed it down with a slurp of lager Shandy. Took a puff on menthol cigarette as we walked into Astro's beer garden. The smoking zone. Despite it pissing down with rain and a bitter wind blowing it was more packed than the inside of the pub.
'What at one of them dating sites, like?' I said.
'Naw, fuckoff, fuckoff, fuckoff. It was on that twattin Shitfacebook. A page for fans of the old Hammer horror film 'n' that. ARSEHOLES!'
'How'd you get to actually meet her, then?'
'Twat said she'd never actually twattin met a twattin, twattin, twattin, twattin Tourette's twat in real life and me being the real fuckin I am and that. Friggin' said she's writing a CUNT book about outsiders or some shite twat shite.'
'Did you shag her?' I gave him a cheeky wink.
'Fuckin naw I twattin didn't. Didn't fuck get a fuckin sniff. Fuckin knocked one out after she fuckin left, like.'

'So, how the fuck did you find out she was a cannibal? Not exactly something that pops up in conversation, like, is it?'

'Well, that's the weird fuckin thing. I was poppin me meds like and then she did the same. So I friggin asked her what the shit hit she was takin and she said the TWAT pills were to supress her friggin SHITE appetite.'

'Yeah, but it's still not something you talk about is it?'

'Friggin aye but she was mixing her twattin meds with tequila wasn't she? Daft friggin cow. Was off her friggin head in no fuckin time. Blabbin on and on and that. ARSE.'

I noticed that John had finished his drink.

'Fancy another?' I said.

'Wouldn't fuckin say no!'

I headed back inside and went to the bar.

'Same again?' said Simon.

'Aye,' I said. 'But slip a little U-Boat in John's, eh? Cheer up his no end.'

'Vodka?'

'Aye. Just the cheap stuff though.'

I headed back with the drinks and carefully placed them on a knee high stone wall.

'Have you got an address for this lass than?' I said.

'Aye, fuckin, aye. But it's all twattin confidential, eh?'

I nodded and waited for the booze to kick in.

***

Herbert Walker was certainly no George Clooney, that was for sure. He had a weird unabrow thing going on, a Mr Spock hairstyle and a boil in the middle of his forehead. The whole thing made him look like a full on psychopath which was more than fair enough since that's exactly what he was. He also sweated profusely and he always looked like he was going to explode into a violent rage any minute. At the moment that was actually true.

'Am I a bitch,' he said, pacing my flat's spare bedroom. 'Do I look like a bitch?'

I resisted the temptation to say 'what?' since I wasn't too sure weather Herbert was quoting Pulp Fiction or just being particularly unoriginal.

'Naw you don't,' I said. I was stood in my Danger Mouse boxer shorts, draining the remains of a can of Carling. A grey dawn was breaking and dirty rain was battering the bedroom window.

Herbert and Tonto- his skinhead minder- had arrived in the middle of the night in order to shake me up. Catch me unawares. But as long as I had a drink in my hand, nothing really shook me up.

'So, why are you trying to shag me like a bitch, then?' he said, winking at Tonto in a way that made my flesh crawl.

'I'm not I ...'

'Three friggin months' rent you owe, twat features,' he said, jabbing a finger at my forehead and reminding me of Fuck-Off John. I wondered if they were related.

'Tomorrow,' I said. 'I'll give you it all tomorrow. One hundred percent.'

[23]

'One hundred and fifty percent,' said Tonto, looking in his little black note book, tapping it with a stubby betting shop ballpoint pen.

'The full whack?' said Herbert, not quite believing what he'd heard.

'Yep,' I said, getting a bit of a glow on from the lager. 'The full Monty. I've some dosh coming my way tomorrow.'

'Ere, when you say tomorrow do you mean today or ... tomorrow?' said Tonto, looking out of the window and the melting night.

'Let's say same time tomorrow, then. So there's no confusion,' I said.

Herbert nodded.

'Make the deal,' he said.

Tonto grabbed me by the throat and dragged me across the room, slamming me against a rickety wardrobe. My glasses flew off my face and the wardrobe door came off its hinges and clattered to the threadbare carpet.

'Fuck up and I'll fuck you up,' he said, patting my arse.

If ever there was motivation ...

***

Although the black leather cat suit was a prominent feature of my childhood television viewing, Emma Peel from The Avengers making a particularly strong impression, I'd never actually seen anyone wear one in real life. But Rhiannon certainly looked the part, though the accent left a lot to be desired. Rather than being Welsh she was actually from Barnsley.

'It were me dad,' she said, puffing on what seemed like her one millionth cigarette since we'd met. We were walking along the sea front, near the lighthouse. The wind blew heavily and rainclouds battered the grey sky. Rhiannon's black raincoat fluttered like a bat's wings.

'He ran a butchers shop and me ma worked at the awld giffs home. Times were 'ard after that Thatcher snatched the mines. And the awldies were droppin' like flies. So, it just seemed like … well … an opportunity. It were just recycling, really. Very ecological.'

'And you still get a craving for it?

She took a can of Special Brew from her back pack. Popped it open.

'Aye. Once you get a taste, there's no goin' back. Not that much, mind you. But every now and again.'

'Where do you get it from?'

She licked her lips.

'That's my little secret?'

She tapped her nose.

'Can't be easy getting … supplies,' I said.

'Well, there's always something for sale on the internet but y'know a lot of that's just scams'

'How do you prepare it when you get it,' I said.

'That's no problem. Me dad taught me the lot. Came in handy, it did. I have a few specialist clients with a taste for choice cuts.'

'And they pay well?' I say. I stamped my feet as we stood next to cannon that was pointing out at sea.

'Top dollar.'

[25]

'So, how would you feel if I told you that I
knew how to get you a new supply? Would
you be interested?'
'Oh, I'd be very interested indeed.'
I took out my mobile and phoned my brother.
Bri, I need a bit of a favour,' I said. I heard him
sigh.
'No, it's not money this time,' I said. And told
him what I needed.

***

Two rivet guns and a roll of fishing line can do
more damage than you'd think, as long as
your reactions are sharp. And I was sharp as a
razor as Herbert and Tonto stormed into my
darkened flat, tripped over the fishing wire
and collapsed face first onto the floor. I shot
them both in the forehead before they knew
what was happening and that was that, really.
I covered the floor with tarpaulin, rolled the
corpses in it and phoned Rhiannon. I could
hear her salivating over the phone. She
turned up half an hour later with a grubby old
transit van and we took the bodies to her
butcher's shop in Barnsley. It really was a lot
easier than you would have thought. As
Rhiannon got to work preparing the special
cuts, I fell asleep on the sofa in the cramped
flat she had above the shop.
A thunder crack awoke me from a deliciously
delirious dream. It was mid-afternoon and
the world seemed to be filled with the smell
of burning flesh. I stretched and got
unsteadily to my feet. Walked into the kitchen

to see Rhiannon eating a massive bacon sarnie.

'Fancy a bite?' she said.

'No, no thanks ... I ...'

But it was too late, I knew. My stomach rumbled like a Russian tank.

'Oh, why not,' I said. 'It's always good to broaden your horizons.'

Two

I close the door, leaving the nutter sweating behind it. His hands dancing and his face twitching. A predatory smile in his eyes. As the latch clicks into place he rushes forward, and slams a heavy palm against the metal. The corridor enjoys a moment of quiet.

"You'll not last long, cunt," he growls, "next time I see you I'll eat your fuckin' spleen."

I fight the urge to throw up, and place my back to the door, allowing the damp steel to cool me. Again Brazill thumps it.

"I know you're still there, I can smell you. Let us out," he says. I don't respond. Another slam. "I'm fuckin' starved here!"

Again I don't respond. And I feel myself slowly lowering to the floor. My arse touching the cold concrete. Behind the door I hear Brazill do the same.

"You can do without one of those kidneys, you know?" he says.

I watch a moth try to satiate its instinct for chasing light by half-heartedly head butting the faint glow emanating from the plastic casing of the emergency lighting.

"You can live a full and decent life with only one arm, maybe even both arms," he says.

The moth moves into the shadows in search of a more satisfying burn. The tip tap of its wings disintegrates into the ether.

"Have you ever heard of Prince Randian?" he asks.

The moth returns from the dark, a glutton for punishment. I ought to snuff it out. Show it that there's really no reward for tenacity in the grand scheme. That would be a wonderful life lesson for its handful of days in existence. There's no point trying because you'll only fail. Take that, Mr Moth.

Suddenly the darkness of the corridor around me is illuminated. The moth is unexpectedly spoilt for choice, and proves me completely wrong. *Well, shut my mouth. Take that, Mr Me.* The lights above my head flicker into life into a jerky, jittery, laboured manner. The ones further up the hall remain dead. Again the bangs and clattering burst into life. An American voice hollers. I don't know enough of Yank accents to even begin to place a region on it. But it calls out. Mentions pills or something. I don't know. He could be asking for *peels.* No, I don't know either. A Scottish baritone threat rides over the American. Shouts *fruity farts* or something. I don't like it. I always found that there was no threat more unnerving than one from a Scotsman. A Scottish woman's voice then admonishes somebody named Paul. Then Keith, again. Already I know his scream. I don't belong here. I should be somewhere else. I should be. I don't really know.

The clank of a door opening awakens me from my prison of noise. Shunts me into action. Benny. He looks to up at the ceiling hopefully before his head drops in despair. "Damn, is that all I fixed?" he asks, his head nodding up to the two lights above me that are working.

"It seems so," I call out, trying to raise my voice above the cacophony of the inmates. Residents. Lunatics. The ten or more voices

[29]

which all fight for prominence. Benny approaches me.

"Don't shout, you'll set them off again," he says.

"But-"

I start to loudly retort about the level of the volume but it's not there. The noise. It's gone. From nowhere to nothing. The corridor is silent but for my own heavy breathing. I'm standing. I don't remember standing up. I search the floor for a memory of when I rose, but it's in vain. Benny smiles.

"Hey, what's the first sign of madness?" he chuckles.

"'Talking to yourself?" I respond, it's obviously not going to be his Suggs punchline again.

"Nah, hairs on the palm of your hand," he says as I instantly spin my hands over to check them.

"You know the second sign?" he asks.

I shake my head, still scrutinising my palms.

"Looking for 'em!" he laughs, and I self-consciously slide my hands instantly into my pocket, a sheepish look on my face. He's fucking hilarious. My eyes drop back to the floor looking for the memory of when I stood up. It isn't there.

"You alright?" he asks, a concern in his eyes. I nod. "It fucks with your head doesn't it? I was the same when I first started, mate. Don't worry about it. You're doing fine. How many did you see?"

"Just one," I say, nodding toward Brazill's door behind me. Benny chuckles.

"Oh, Paul, eh? Yeah, he's an experience."

"I heard that, *Benny*," says the muffled voice of Paul Brazill, dropping a slick emphasis at the end. My colleague thumps the door. "Back in the corner, fucker. Or you'll go hungry all night."

I don't completely understand Benny's relationship with these people. He swears at them. Threatens them. Is that even allowed? Surely this is some sort of human rights infringement. He sees the concern flicker into my eyes and shakes his head.

"He won't go hungry," he says, "but you have to know what pushes their buttons to get them to behave," he says, "simple behavioural control is all."

"Who's Prince Randian?" I ask.

"Look, these lights aren't gonna fix themselves. I called it in but they can't get anybody here until the morning, so we're gonna have to do what we can ourselves."

He nods to the torch in my hand. I don't remember him passing it to me, but he must have done. "That should keep you happy enough until I come back. We still need to check on the boys. Do you want me to get you started?"

Alphabet Man

By Craig Furchtenicht

Darkness.

Oh, for Christ sake! There goes the damn lights again. I swear this place gets more rundown by the day. How's a guy supposed to get any work done in this kind of environment? First it was the boiler system and then the water. Now this? They could at least fire up some axillary lights so I can finish my painting, my masterpiece. Getting the details just right in the hair is hard enough to do with finger paints, let alone in the dark.

They used to let me use real paint. Not this worthless non-toxic third grade crap, but real paints. Of course that was before the little incident with the previous activities counsellor. Maybe it was the one before her, I really can't remember now. Either way, the ones after her know better than to mispronounce my last name. Seeing a #6 Filbert brush protruding from the weepy mess that used to be their colleague's eyeball tends to make people enunciate German surnames quite fluently. Now they simply address me by my first name, Craig. Some call me Alphabet.

Timing around here is frigging unbelievable. Just as I was getting ready to put the final touches on my L'art du jour and then Whammo, pitch black. The lights go out and the screaming begins, accompanied by the steady drumming of fists against eleven other doors just like mine. Like chimps at the zoo before feeding time, this bunch. I swear I'm the only fucking sane one in this godforsaken place.

This couldn't have happened a few hours ago when the sadistic bastards in the kitchen were hard at it, screwing up something as simple as beans and franks. Last time the power cut out was an hour before supper. The kitchen staff had to scramble to whip up something that didn't require cooking yet fell within the dietary guidelines set forth by our blessed health department. We had peanut butter and jelly sandwiches. Tasted like shit but made for some strikingly interesting earth tones when blended with paint.

Tonight we got the old death by beans and franks. They serve it four times a week here at Saint David's. Never used to be half bad until they stopped serving it with the entire frank still intact. I don't know the whole story, but I heard they had to rush a guy down the hall from me to the infirmary after he tried to cram two franks into his "prison purse" and they got stuck. I guess he kept it to himself for about a week until his bowels nearly ruptured. Now we eat our supper meats neatly trimmed into manageable bite-sized portions like a bunch of halfwits.

Now I don't know this for a fact and I'll deny it if you quote me, but I'm fairly certain that the sausage sneaker was in fact one Mr. Bracha. I only suspect this on account of a debt he owed me after a card game in the day room last month. My straight flush had cost him a dozen lorazepam. Like any honorable man with poor card playing skills, he promptly paid me at the first opportunity. I'm not saying that this is absolutely indisputable evidence, but when he pulled the small baggie of pills from his keister the whole lot reeked strongly of shit and faintly of hot dogs. Oh well, to each his own.

That reminds me. I've not seen one member of the lovely staff for over an hour. The doctors are

[33]

usually gone this time of the night, but the place is usually teeming with nurses and orderlies. They hover around the desk near the unit entrance, impatiently waiting to dumb us down with meds or ruin somebodies night with a round of unethical therapy sessions. They know how I get when I don't get my prescribed dosage on time. If this keeps up I might have to resort to dipping into my own stash, stink and all.

Wait. Footsteps.

Two pairs, reverberating off of the linoleum like choreographed thunder. I recognize the tubby night watchman's labored breathing as he slowly approaches, but have no clue who the second set belongs to. Peering through the glassless metal grate that serves as my window does me little good. It's so dark that I can't even see my own paint slathered hands in front of my face, but I can almost taste the cheap dollar store aftershave he faithfully drowns himself in before work each night.

"What the fuck, Fat ass? Who forgot to pay the light bill?" I shout out to a face I cannot see. I know he's there because the vapors from his smell good burn at my useless eyeballs. "I need my pills, like now!"

"Settle down, Alphabet. Just the electric. Not the end of the world. Get in the corner, cunt." For a moment there is only silence except for faint shuffling of feet on the other side of my door. There's an awkward glory hole quality about the muted pause. Finally he adds, "New guy this is Craig. Craig meet new guy. He'll hold down the fort while I figure out what's going on with the damn lights."

"Uh, hello," a meek voice trickles in through the grate. Sounds young and scared. This could be interesting. I don't get much in the way of interesting in here. Before I can reply a shrill scream echoes through the hallway.

"And don't give him any shit while I'm gone." The fat one's footsteps click down the hall as he beats feet out of the unit. His steps come to a halt just shy of the exit and his booming voice rips through the unlit air. "That's goes for all of you cunts."

Left alone with a cherry guard during a blackout. Oh the fun I could have. I strain to get a better look through the window when a harsh beam of light erupts through the opening, erasing the blackness and sending me scrambling backwards. I rub at my eyes without thinking and instantly feel the tacky wetness of the paint as it smears all over my face.

"Goddamn! What are you trying to do, frigging blind me for good?"

"Uh, sorry about that." A nervous clearing of his throat leads to another uncomfortable silence. Finally he directs his flashlight over my shoulder to the easel behind me. "Painting, eh?"

I press my multicolored face to the grate and snarl, "No shit. Now what gave you that idea, newbie?"

He backs up with a gasp and the flashlight tumbles to the unforgiving hardness of the linoleum. Immediately the bulb blinks out with a crack and it's back to total darkness. "Fuck's sake," he mutters to himself.

I say nothing until I'm certain that I can mask the pleasure in my voice over his dilemma. "Hey newbie, I used to be an electrician before I came here. Open the door and I'll get this dump lit back up in no time. What do you say?"

"Don't do it," a voice echoed from further down the corridor. There is an uneasy wavering to it that makes me think of overstretched rope. "We're not supposed to be out of our rooms after lights out."

So much for that idea. The slim chance of the newbie actually springing me loose go from slim to absolute nil when Edgerton decides to open his big yap. Damn conformist. Guy won't even shit without being told to.

"Thanks, but I don't think that'd be a good idea," the newbie replies. "Get in the corner."

"Yeah, Fruity-farts. Relax yoursel'. You're no afraid ay the dark are ya?"

"Shut the fuck up Wilson, you cock smoker," I scream. Bastard always knows what buttons to push. Every day he comes up with some new and irritating way to butcher my name. "You'll see how goddamn scared of the dark I am when I bite off your fucking eyelids at breakfast tomorrow."

The guard murmurs, still fumbling to resuscitate his dead flashlight. I can feel the nervous tension oozing from his pores even with the heavy door between us. Then his breathing escalates into rapid Lamaze-like puffs. "Fuck's sake. You're the one who blinded the therapist with the paintbrush. You're him."

"Yep, that would be me," I confess. "I'd sign you an autograph but they won't let me have pens anymore. Too sharp and pointy."

"Fuck's sake," he repeats.

The shrill screams from down the hall evolve into a cacophony of barks. The sound pierces my frontal lobes like a dentist drill to the forehead. I tell you, that goddamned Keith and his barking are enough to drive a sane man over the edge. I hate that even worse that someone mucking up my name.

"That's Keith. Feel free to rubber hose him when nobody's watching," I suggest. "I won't tell."

"Thanks, I suppose." The newbie lets out a jittery laugh, then his face hardens. "Brazill told me his story. It was fucked up. You think you can top it? Why would you blind somebody?"

I stare into the dark, trying to decide if he's just making small talk or if he really wants to know. It's a stupid question either way. The proper one would have been, what wouldn't make a guy want to do something like that. I sit on the edge of my mattress and sigh. My painting's a wash and I've got nothing but time to kill before sleep catches up to me. So why not fuck with the kid's mind a bit and tell him what brought me to this fine little house of horrors.

First of all, I was not always the unwashed wretch that I appear to be now. Back in my better days I was a regular guy with normal ambitions that didn't involve blinding therapists or winning impossibly easy hands at poker from drooling imbeciles. Try to keep that in mind a few years from now when they finish molding you into just another hack prick like the rest of them.

I wasn't really an electrician back then, but rather a letter carrier. You know, a mailman. Didn't even paint before coming here. That was my wife's thing, not mine. Damn good at it too. Enough to make a decent chunk of change for some of her better pieces. We did okay. House too big for the two of us, nice cars in the drive and most of all each other. Everything was going great until that fucking little rat dog came into our lives.

I don't know if it was empty-nest-syndrome or just an artsy phase Amy was going through. I didn't even know she liked dogs until I came home from work one day and stepped in a puddle of its piss as soon as I kicked off my shoes and walked into the living room. There the little fucker was, sitting there in *my* favorite chair. I'm peeling a piss soaked sock from my foot and this smug little ball of fur was nonchalantly licking his own dick on the seat of the chair that I'd been looking forward to plopping my ass in the minute I walked in the door.

"Amy!" I yelled, hopping on one foot to the laundry room. I dropped the sock into the hamper and poked my head into the spare bedroom we had converted into her studio. "Honey, what the hell is that in my chair?"

My wife completed several strokes with her brush before setting it on the shelf below her easel. She stood up and walked out of the room, almost passing through me like I wasn't even there. No, how was your day, honey? Or, what do you want for supper? No nothing. She just waddled her age plumped ass into the living room and hovered over the dog, who was still busy going to town on his little red boner like nobody's business. Amy leaned down and plucked the dog from the chair and held it up to me. "This is Scooter. He's a miniature Schnauzer. Isn't he gorgeous?"

"I guess, but didn't you think to discuss it with me before getting a dog?" I asked. Scooter stared at me and let out a soft growl, his fire engine hued crotch missile twitching between his dangling legs. I let out a disgusted burp and added, "You know I'm slightly allergic, right?"

Amy pulled the dog back and held it up to her face. "That's only if we don't keep you clean. Isn't that right, Scooter baby? Him's a clean boy, isn't he?" She proceeded to rub her nose into the dogs face until he reciprocated with a flurry of licks to her chin and mouth.

"Jeez, Ames. Didn't you just see where that things tongue was?" I said, repulsed to the point of nausea.

"Oh, Craig. Don't be such a stick in the mud. A dog's mouth is ten times cleaner than a human mouth." She set the dog on the floor and smiled as it curiously circled my legs. "Look, he's getting to know you."

It sniffed my toes for a second, let out a low growl and then proceeded to furiously hump the top of my foot. His furry puppy ass pumped up and down as he wrapped his front paws around my ankle in a death grip. I shrieked involuntarily and shook my leg in a whip-crack motion sending the horny little beast tumbling across the carpet. It looked up at me scornfully before resuming its previous business of self-fellatio.

"Yeah, he's getting to know me alright."

Amy shot me a sour look, grabbed Scooter up from the floor and headed toward the bedroom, cooing nonsensically to the dog as she went. As my wife disappeared around the corner carrying my new worst nightmare in her arms I stared down at my foot as if it were a shameless whore.

I know what you're thinking, newbie. It's just a puppy, they do that. But that obscene violation was just the tip of the proverbial iceberg. From that point forward I became a second class citizen in my own house. To a sexually deviant dog with a foot fetish no less.

I spent the night locked out of the bedroom and ended up sleeping on the couch. I woke up some time before dawn to the sound of ripping fabric. I fumbled for the lamp switch only to find Scooter dragging the jacket of my postal uniform across the living room floor. Tattered remnants of what used to

[39]

be the left sleeve trailed behind him as he went. I heaved a cushion in his direction, barely missing him. The little bastard just looked up for a moment, hiked up his leg and let loose on the carpet.

This was how my morning started. This was how my life after Scooter began.

It didn't stop there, getting foot-raped or losing dibs on my favorite recliner. Nor was it being a captive audience to Scooter's perpetual lick fest on the cushion of said chair. Disgusting as that was, I could have tolerated it if that was all there was. I was even getting used to the pissy smell that my socks had gradually taken on. I think what bothered me more than anything was sharing the bed that used to be half mine. I was lucky to get half a pillow after Scooter took over.

Ever wake up to the smell of dog farts, newbie? No? You're a lucky man.

Going to work was my only reprieve. I enjoyed my job. Only now I did it half as efficiently and twice as slow due to the high doses of over-the-counter allergy medication I took to keep from sneezing every two minutes. Amy had abandoned her knack for churning out gallery worthy pieces to spend her days painting canvas after canvas of her furry little muse. She insisted on hanging them all over the house. In lieu of cleaning and cooking she spent her spare time parading Scooter around the neighborhood in cute little outfits that she ordered online.

A wonderful cook for the first twenty years of our marriage, Amy took as much pride in detail and presentation of meals as she did with her art. Never once did I come home from a hard day of delivering mail, wondering if there would be a hearty meal waiting for me. Three months after Scooter arrived, I was eating microwavable frozen dinners while he dined on five dollar a can dog food. The meat in that stuff looked more realistic than the rubbery processed crap they put in my meals. She even served him on the fancy plates we used to reserve only for special occasions.

Day after day. Week after week. It was always the Scooter show at the Furchtenicht residence, 24/7. Not a word came out of Amy's mouth that didn't involve some cutesy thing that the dog had done during the course of the day. It got to the point where she stopped talking directly to me, but through the dog instead.

"Tell daddy what you did today, baby. Momma is so proud of you. Uh huh, yes her is." Always followed by that gross exchange of Eskimo kisses from her and a tongue bath from him. Each time I was subjected to their disgusting displays of affection, the more I wanted to strangle them both.

My lack of fondness for the dog was not lost on Amy. She tried to placate me by assuring me that I wasn't being replaced. She said she just needed something to fill the void left after our daughter had moved out. I knew better. The only void she had was the rapidly growing dead space between her ears. That mutt was filling it back in with enough "adorable" to make a sane person want to puke.

The biggest shock to me came during the week before my birthday. Amy greeted me at the door, smiling so widely that I initially thought she might be having a stroke. She told me that there was something she wanted to show me. She led me into our bedroom and told me to close my eyes with a hint of nervousness in her voice. I sighed impatiently and obliged, absolutely not knowing what to expect.

For once Scooter was off doing his own thing instead of tailing my wife like a constant shadow. I won't lie. The sound of fabric sliding over skin combined with the notion of having her in the bedroom all to myself ignited a spark in my nether regions that I hadn't felt in a long time.

"Okay you can open them now," she whispered.

I couldn't believe what I was seeing. Amy was stark naked and sprawled out across the bed. Needless to say I was highly aroused. My pecker hadn't seen action since the four-legged monster had invaded our lives. Like any sex-starved husband I immediately dropped trou and was ready to go before she changed her mind. She gasped as I entered her, further escalating my excitement.

Then she threw a curve ball by pushing me away long enough to roll over on all fours. In our twenty years of lovemaking we had never once graduated past the missionary position. Rather than questioning her spontaneous urge to experiment I went for it with unbridled vigor. That was when I first saw the tattoo.

Below the small of her back and just above the crack of her ass was a photo realistic, full color tattoo of none other than him. Fucking Scooter staring up at me with that subtle tilt of his head and those watery doggy eyes. I was instantly as limp as a wet noodle. At this point I would have had an easier time shoving toothpaste back into the tube than finishing what my wife and I had started. Nothing kills a good hard-on like a tramp stamp of a puppy inked just above your wife's ass.

I almost bit my tongue in half as the unspeakable happened. I'm staring down at my Judas penis when I felt Scooter's cold wet nose burrowing nostril deep into my asshole. I let out a scream and rolled out from behind Amy, off the side of the bed. Scooter barely had time to register the danger he was in before I backhanded him straight off the bed. He landed with a yelp and scurried out of the room.

"Scooter," Amy screamed. Her stunned look told me that I may just as well have struck her instead. She jumped down and ran after the whimpering man molester.

We never spoke of it again. Hell, we rarely spoke at all until the following weekend, the day of my birthday party. Amy had invited several of my co-workers and their wives weeks before the incident in the bedroom. Cancelling was out of the question. We played the part of the happy couple and gracious hosts to our utmost ability. The food was great and the wine did well to ease the underlying tension between us. It went good until Scooter crashed the party.

Of course Amy had outdone herself, dressing Scooter in a cutesy doggy mailman outfit for the benefit of my supervisor and the other guys. Everyone got a big chuckle out of it and the wives doted over the little fleabag to the point of absurdity. Scooter sensed the overabundance of attention and strutted around poolside like the cock of the walk. Then he developed a deep infatuation with my sandals.

Several times I found myself propping my feet up on a chair or dangling them over the edge of the pool just to keep the little shit from doing anything vile in front of the guests. No matter how I positioned myself the sick freak never took his eyes off of my partly exposed feet for more than a few seconds. I tried to get Amy to lock him inside the house but she refused.

[43]

"Oh grow up and stop being so jealous of the dog. Everyone's paying attention to the birthday boy too," she said with a happy wife grin masking the contempt in her voice. "Go talk to your boss. Maybe you'll manage to get a raise for your birthday. God knows that's the only thing you have a chance of getting up these days."

No lie, newbie. She really said that to me.

She gravitated back to the ladies after freshening up everyone's drinks. I joined the men and did my best to shake the sting out of my bruised ego. The conversation evolved from the weather to football to badmouthing a few co-workers that didn't make it to the party. I was building up enough nerve and blood alcohol content to spring the idea of a pay increase to my supervisor when it happened.

Taking full advantage of the lapse in my defensive manoeuvres, Scooter targeted my right foot and moved in for the attack. The moment I felt his paws grip my ankle and the warmth of his thing snake its way under my sandal strap, I jerked my foot back in hopes of going unnoticed. Much to my horror the dog let out a blood-curdling squeal. Even in all my years at St. David's, I've never heard a sound like that come out of any living thing. A lump formed in the pit of my gut when I realized what had happened. His dick was stuck in the metal buckle of my sandal.

Amy screamed and rushed forward, followed by an entourage of empathetic women. She glared at me as if it were my fault and carefully spent an agonizing ten minutes separating her darling puppy's penis from the hardware of my sandal. I tried once to suggest my taking the sandal off but was vetoed after the decibel level of Scooter's cries intensified. By the time the extraction was completed the women were all crying and the men doubled over with laughter. I was going to be the butt of every dick and dog joke at the post office from then until the day I retired.

"Goddamn, First-Dick. No wonder your feet stink so bad when you walk past my office in the morning," my supervisor Don snorted through a mouthful of artichoke dip. Tears streamed down the curves of his fat face.

I stared down at the source of everything that was wrong in my life. Spots of blood stained his outfit and the tip of his cock, which he was almost certain to start going to town on any minute. The mixture of crying and laughter buzzed in my brain until I simply lost it.

I don't think anyone saw me walk away and go into the garage. I'm pretty certain nobody saw me come back out with the 15 ounce claw hammer in my hand and I'm positive that none of them expected what would happen next.

The crowd of women around Scooter parted like the red sea as my bare foot swept through and connected with his back end. You should have seen it, newbie. Like a fucking football, the little shit flew through the air and splashed down in the middle of the swimming pool. He tried to swim but he must have been half paralyzed, 'cause he just swam around in circles with the one side of him that still worked. The wives screamed while their drunk husbands jumped in to play the hero. Can you imagine, half a dozen mailmen trying to save a dog of all things?

Amy stopped crying long enough to run over and slap my face, screaming that I had "gone too far this time." My eyes shifted from her angry glare to the chaotic scene around us. The drowning dog in the pool, the screaming postal wives and their wannabe hero husbands. Then to the hammer. I don't know why, but before I had time to think about it the claw

[45]

end was buried into the side of her head. I stood there, wondering what the fuck I had just done.

Someone screamed and I snapped out of the initial shock of braining my wife of twenty years. I surveyed the stunned faces of all my party guests and pulled the end of the hammer out of Amy's skull. She collapsed to the patio below her with a meaty thud. Everyone started yelling bloody murder and I guess I just went into survival mode.

I was a God that day. Not Craig, the second class husband. Not the mediocre mailman with stinky feet and a name too long to say right. Or the object of some perverted mutt's sick foot fetish. I was the mighty defender of my own fractured dignity. I took it all back from them, one beautiful swing of the hammer at a time.

Some fought back. Most just closed their eyes waited for the end to come. Like baby seals in the North Arctic they were. Just flopping around the edge of the pool, waiting their turn to get the club. They all screamed a little as I helped them feel my pain. I circled the perimeter of the pool and dispatched them one by one. They tried to claw their way out of the pool, but the concrete around the edge was too slicked up with the blood of their wives to get a decent hold. I don't know how long it took, but the screaming eventually stopped.

Words cannot describe the feeling of relief that came over me just then. Sure I was exhausted and covered in the blood of people I could hardly stand. But looking at them, floating in the pinkish water, a quality of mutual serenity fell over the backyard that most people rarely get to share with others. I sipped from a glass of wine and watched Scooter's aimless paddling wind to a stop. I smiled for the first time in months as the wet fabric of his little mailman costume weighted his lifeless body and he drifted to the bottom of the pool.

So there you have it, newbie. That's how I punched my ticket to the looney bin. I guess the answer to your question is simple. You know, about why I would blind someone with a paintbrush or plan to bite Wilson's eyelids off before breakfast in the morning. They won't let us keep hammers at St. David's, that's why.

Now go bother somebody else for a while. I need to get some sleep so I can finish my painting when the lights decide to come back on. You know what they say, practice makes perfect. One of these days I might even get the shape of the eyes right. Little bastard did have the cutest damn eyes.

Three

I slide the grate closed, leaving *Furchtenicht* to his painting. Beside his door there's his black name slate. Under the oddly spelled name, somebody has chalked in *Thirsty Nick* and scribbled a winking face. It seems his name draws a lot of scope for mispronunciation. I make a conscious decision to say it the same as he did for the rest of the time I'm here. He seemed affable enough though. For a lunatic. From the other side of the door I hear him muttering about a *fuckin' dog* some more, before I step away from his room. There are six more on this floor. In one of them a woman cries. Benny said nothing about women in here. The cries are coming from across the hall. Although the experience with Furchtenicht has hardened my confidence, I don't want to investigate *that* just yet. I'm still not sure I'd have a leg to stand on as far as insurance went if I was attacked by one of these oddballs. Maybe that's unfair. Brazill, for his cannibalistic ways and his unnerving penchant for harvesting me with his imagination, seemed okay. He was comprehendible enough. The Yank, Craig, was the same. I know what it is more than anything, that's fucking with my head. It's this fucking building. Every corner creeps me out. Every surface is slick with threat. The fact that I haven't seen a single other person than Benny, and these people that live here. Surely to God there would be *somebody* else with some sort of medical, or psychological, or even fucking philosophic qualification. Benny and I, we're guards. That's it. We're here to preserve peace. Maybe in the day it's different. Maybe we've simply not hit the real staff quarters yet, and somewhere above us there's a floor that's just teeming with doctors. Maybe. I won't hold my breath.

Above me the light flickers into life. Inside the plastic casing a thousand flies' corpses tip tap against it as the vibration kick-starts their disco of the dead. Again it is only above me. Down the hall the moth pings against the ceiling on the hunt for a fresh glow. I half expect Benny to come lumbering into my airspace again, but a few minutes of waiting proves fruitless, and I move on. The next door has no grated window like the last one did. It's more like Brazill's. The first. A solid steel chunk that protects me from the man behind it. Or vice versa. On the wall is the name slate. *Godwin, Richard.* My fist is balled and knocking against the metal before I've even made the decision to do it.

"Get in the corner," I say, "I'm here to fix the lights." There's no noise from the room. "Did you hear me?" Nothing.

"I need to you to get in the corner," I say, again. I bring the keys up, and after a brief jingling I find the one with *RG* etched upon in with a fine point marker pen. I continue a mantra instructing the man in the room to get into the corner, and that I'm here with every intention of repairing his lighting situation. The edge of the key tickles the mouth of the lock, and after a couple of nervous prods against the cold metal, like a teenage virgin poking indiscriminately at his first love's crotch on the maiden voyage into the sexual sea, it finds its sweet spot and slides into the barrel.

"Get in the corner," I say, my right hand twisting the key, sliding the bolt from its slumber, "I'm here to fix the lights."

Still I hear nothing from the room. I pull the key from the lock and attach the bunch to my belt.

"Get in the corner," I say, my right hand grabbing a firm hold of the handle, applying pressure to it, "I'm here to fix the lights."

My left hand holds the torch. Conscious this time of inadvertently blinding a man that I'm here to protect.

"Get in the corner," I say, using my elbow to gently push the door open, "I'm here-"

BANG.

The door is slammed closed in front of me with a force. The metal smacks me hard against the cheek, and a dull throb aches as I pick myself up from the floor. The torch has skittered away along the corridor and casts an odd light against the wall in the darkness. My imagination throws a rapid pair of legs flashing through the powerful beam into the equation, and that familiar shudder makes its ascent from the base of my spine to the crook of my neck once again. That wasn't anything. I saw nothing. I made it up. Of course I did. I have the keys to every door in here, and they're all locked. *Keep it to-fucking-gether!* I collect my torch and approach the door again. With an apprehension that sits on another level to the last time I place my hand once again on the handle.

"Get," I say, "in the corner."

My hand pressures the handle.

"I'm here to fix the lights."

This time the pressure is in vain. The man on the other side holds it against its will.

"I know why you're here," a voice says, "and I won't allow it."

The voice sounds southern. Cockney London maybe. I don't know. Anything south of Birmingham sounds exactly the same to me.

"I'm here to help," I say, "to fix the lights."

"You're here to fuck me," he says. I'm really not here to fuck him. "I know who you are. You won't fuck me." "I promise, I'm not going to fuck you. Just. Get in the corner. Please."

"Enter this room and you will be sorry. Do your deeds. Replace *the other* all you want. But you stay away, do you hear?"

I push the knob again but it's no use. He's too strong. He's obviously a lot more determined to keep me out than I am to get in there. Benny didn't tell me what to do in this situation, but I'm guessing if this Godwin fella is intent on his alone time, then I should just move on.

"Okay," I say, "I'll stay out."

I take the keys from my belt again, and find his, before locking the door with less apprehension than I had when I unlocked it. I move to walk away, but am halted by the voice.

"Wait."

"Okay?"

Nothing happens. I sigh. These people.

"What?"

"At your feet."

I look down. There's a curled sheet of paper or two, pushed out from beneath the door and pressed against my feet. As I stoop to collect it I hold the torch on the papers. On them there are lines and lines, all in a deep red which is turning almost brown. The ink from one of the symbols flakes away beneath my touch. My eyes scan the patterns. Nothing much of it makes sense. The patterns are almost words, but not really.

"What's this?" I ask the door, "Your homework?"

"Don't be facetious, *replicant*. Here."

Another something slides from beneath the door. A mirror.

[51]

"Are you allowed that?"

"Would I have it if I weren't?"

I shrug to concede the point, and stoop to collect the mirror.

"Now," he says, "read, replicant."

PORCUPINES

BY RICHARD GODWIN

THE PORCUPINES wept black ink when they brought me here. I am fettered like Harcamone at Fontrevault, a revolutionary with a massive rose beating in the place of my heart, less madman than visionary, reduced by the dumb indifference of man. And if you don't know what brought me to this place then you too deserve their spikes.

I travel the grey city at night, I stagger into the leprous dawn, unbridled, a visitant to your aroused dreams. These walls do not contain me, nor do they swallow the sum of all your fears, for there are twelve of us. That fact seems to have escaped the notice of the blind governor who whistles in his sleep, for I have watched his dreams of teenage girls dressed in human skin while his daughter chokes on his lust in the next room.

I see beneath the ruins of their minds. I know what dark thoughts they refuse to allow entry, and they place us here that they may be free of them, but they will never be free.

We number twelve, don't you see? They are following our book unto the letter, and I hold the spike that I dip into the ink. They have placed the apostles in this place. St David's. The walls are made of sand. I enter the sea, I fetch fish forth for my brothers as they howl at night and the guard wanders the corridors, his skin resembling the texture of leather. They are replacing him. He won't believe me

[53]

when I tell him he is visited at night, he's intent on the porn channels, an addict to the deceit of flesh.

How can they acknowledge that we hold veracity in our hands? Voracious veracity is a crime now. They are the deluded ones. I know the nature of skin.

We live in simulation. These residents of the replaced world echo man and woman. They started with my wife. I saw what they had placed inside her.

Each night their clone visited me. She danced naked, her genitals gaping in insane arousal. And within her sliced peach I saw it swell as she stretched her lips apart. Its head jutted out of her like an obscene clitoris, the penis that inhabits the female body now. They are re-gendering us.

They began replacing skin years ago. Piece by piece they reassembled man and woman until we became this violated mutation. Inside her I see the phallus, it emerges as she spreads her lips, ushering desire into her fetid body, but I didn't yield and so they sent me to this place. Soon the guard will be penetrated from the inside. The skin will become theirs, the cloning complete. The politics of skin is an industry on a vast scale, and we have threatened its profits. But I know how to penetrate them.

The prime minister is feeding on them. He is the detritus of our times. Cloned man. They want our skins. I have told this to countless people while I stand at street corners, a ragged piece of flesh in my hand to prove to you, don't you see? They've replaced our flesh with the factory. They're replacing you as I speak. I howl at my cell.

But I know the porcupines. I penetrate with quills, I urge flesh towards sexual oblivion.

The replicants are breeding. But they do not conjoin in fluids or a blind ecstasy fetched from the tombs of Roman Emperors, they copulate like small black ants beneath the shoes of waitresses while you are served the rotted meat. They are eating you from the inside. The food they serve will corrode your intestines and make you their butter. They will fuck you with their sad and pointless drills, rape your wives and send you to that place of sorrow.

I escaped to the castle of David, for they do not know my brothers are amassing for war here. We have been hired by the one called Bracha, he holds the sword and it is dripping with blood, their blood. I lacerate them with quills, I remove their genitals and place them smouldering on fires and make them eat their offal.

No newspaper will dare utter the truth, that man is extinct, a replicant made of ash. We twelve are the world of flesh. We twelve will revolutionise their black extinct world, I will empty the politicians of their hideous lies with razors sharpened on their small sharp teeth.

They invade our homes. They emptied my wife of her genitals and tried to insert the slithering reptile inside her womb. But I saw the serpent woman at dawn, her gaping cunt spewing semen, gonorrhoea, the legs and arms of sailors washed there by desire, while it erupted from her womb, her cock in the cloned world. This strap on jack lesbian whore screwed by all the politicos, drunk on come in back alleys where the faithful never wander at night. I hacked its head off and threw it to the gulls. And the porcupines came along and ate it.

They showed us the way. All my brothers know, we have sharpened spikes and we pierce the empty flesh and bleed them dry of lies at night.

I've hacked and emptied them of liquid deceit. David was a porcupine and this is our home.

They think they've locked us up but we are there. We dwell on your doorsteps, our hands clutching the spikes.

The only way to tell the flesh is piercing, and the porcupines know the way. I sliced her apart and removed the snake and fed it to them. They smothered it in quills and made it a living writhing thing of meat, for that is all they are, beneath their lies and rhetoric, red raw meat just like the thing that visits you at night when the guard has gone home to his phallic wife. She rapes him in bed. She inserts the serpent in his anus.

George Bernard Shaw told his children he would rather they become prostitutes than politicians. Porcupines know about skin. I know the false skins they wear with their lies and machinations. They want woman to enter the body of man that they may feed upon you, they have phallicised the female that she may penetrate you and bring forth the replicated world. To what do you succumb by dawn? To what lies have you sold your houses? You are being replaced while men touch the soft surfaces of your loved ones, their faces saintly, an apotheosis of sexual sin beneath the guttering candle at your fading windowpane. For they are hired by the cloned world. They defecate on your mattress and feed you sandwiches made of fur. But only the quill knows them. I made them the pin cushion, I emptied them while they spat blood. The porcupines know, with quills I win.

Only the poisoned flowers hang outside these walls, we live in the age of venom. Hypocritical reader, there will be no guillotine here, no hanging, I confess all, into your dumb indifferent ear, while you lick away the crumbs of politics at the breakfast table next to your yawning wife.

This is how it happened. One night I noticed that the prime minister had cameras in his skull, it was apparent to me from the moment I turned on the TV. I told my wife but she laughed. She wouldn't listen to me when I told her he regularly masturbated in supermarket windows waving his semen-dripping cock at passers-by then rounded them up and buggered them routinely before police officers removed their genitals.

The government is collecting genitals. The prime minister has two penises, one he rapes and buggers with, the other he uses to spin his lies, it flickers from his grey mouth like an ill-fitting clitoris, an offensive lump of aroused meat. He is employing a police force of sexless mutants. They never piss, never copulate, beneath their trousers are antennae. He wants to be the father of the new tribe. But the new tribe is not made of man, but clones. Night by night he sends the cock woman to rape you in your sleep, and she carries away your penises and vaginas, your balls and wombs to the place where they manufacture the new world. Empty the politicians of blood, make them paper so we may write our tales upon them, walk wild into the wind, summon all revolutionaries from this band of brothers, unlock the doors and let us take the streets.

I saw her the first night while my wife slept. She entered our room and raised her dress, parted her cunt and put forth the snake, but I lopped his lying head off and inserted it in her anus. She began to crap foul sewage, a river of faeces that stank up the garden. I was accused of burying bodies, do I look like a murderer? Are these a murderer's hands? You may say I carry scars, but I say to you your eyes deceive you in this hollow light.

They failed to remove my genitals. I bore children, I armed them with weapons, and they sent us here. I knew their skins were new. I passed them in the streets, their eyes shone out of the sheer material, there is no flesh left any more out there, the only flesh is here in this place they call a prison, where we watch you all.

I found a way to test their skins. I knew it from the moment they came to me with ink and I began to find the several uses for their quills.

The government tried to exterminate them. All porcupines. But they hid in my cellar. I spoke to them at night in their strange nocturnal language, they told me of the way to discover the true properties of skin. I learned how to unhook and use their spikes. And I dipped them into the cloned flesh.

When the penis woman came again, I skewered her with their quills. I entered her until the chattering lips she used to guile us were like a pin cushion, then I emptied her. I found them out, the females of the hidden cock. I punctured their sick and sleeping lies with the sharp points, and their skins gave way. The world began to see the cloning.

And so they branded me a criminal, insane. What madness made their politics, what dark body do you rise with at dawn when the caterpillars flee from your brain?

With porcupine quills I penetrated the false flesh. I searched for skin in the empty dawns. You cannot remove skin that is covered in spikes. My skin is beyond you, and the weak clutches of your enterprise. For the men who masquerade as leaders are nothing more than imagery. Born of pornography, they seek the eternal object. They want to cover our bodies with their creed, they inscribe us, they write their manifesto on our flesh and sexuality. Only the porcupines know the way to defend man's flesh. Only the porcupines pierce their cloned bodies, and unravel the harnessed sexuality that they fear so much. Crave, crave. Desire the body of woman, penetrate until you know that it is skin you touch and not some vile and alien thing.

I entered them, their bodies yielding to me. I spiked and pierced them until they were nothing more than paper.

I would inscribe them, not be their depository. They want to fill you with semen, own your minds, I say check their genitals at the door.

Of course, it was a clever ruse, to bring in a leader who'd raped hundreds of men and women, a vile pervert who needs to puncture holes all day. Watch him speak, the shit dripping from his phallic tongue while he touches himself beneath the podium. They thought they'd come up with the invisible lie. For who would believe me when I told them?

What happened? Beyond the piercing and the finding out of false flesh? Beyond the discovery there are clones in our streets? Beyond the fact that they have altered you?

I lacerated the cock women. I tore their genitals from them and watched them atrophy like poisoned muscle.

Then one bright morning I fed the prime minister a penis and let himself choke to death on his own orgasms. They wanted to elect me. They sent me here instead, his police were still at large. They placed the bodies of mutilated women in my cellar, hideous deformities full of needles and sharpened objects placed there by a madman. These were the politicians' crimes. Everywhere they are replacing bodies with clones. You do not know because perhaps you are one. They will imprison your, lock you up if you suspect that the women you fuck are fucking you with cocks placed there by them. They want to re-gender us all. They think they can keep me here. But I know the way to the guard's heart. Each night the porcupines visit me with ink. They leave me with quills, they have no need for skin, for by the morning it will be covered with weapons.

My fellow inmates are gathering weapons. We are amassing for war. The guard will be the first to fall. He thinks he is a priest listening to our confessions, taking away his tidy version of us to his tired wife. He pores over documents in his office where we watch him. But he doesn't know that each night he is violated by her, she bears the cloned penis.

She is inseminating him with self-replication. His skin scales away like scabs. We observe him while he labours under the illusion that he is keeping us prisoner. I may well free our guard with quills. I may show him that penetration of skin still living will save him from their vile plans.

The quills unlock the jail. I turn them in the rusting mechanism, let loose my brothers into the streets. They are metal, machetes, all form of war now, we are armed to the teeth and enter your homes to deliver you of the cloned lives you lead. What idle hours do you pass each day digested by the political body?

They say the bodies of punctured women were found beneath my house. They claim their skins were unrecognisable, a shredding of the flesh by a maniac. I say I returned them to their skins, and removed from them the scale of replicants. The porcupines come to me, I ride their smooth backs into the streets, a sailor on a sea of spikes.

Four

The paper drops from my hands. The sheets curl and swirl as gravity does its thing. The first thought that comes to mind is that I'm glad as fuck that I didn't go into his room. If that's what he's scared of, or prepared for, or fuck knows what, then I'm pleased that I'm not in there with him. The second thought is *Bracha.* Furchtenicht mentioned the name, he says he's another nutcase, but now it's there in black, or I suppose red and congealed brown and white. Godwin says he was beckoned here by the man. Once again, I have no fucking clue what is going on here. Is Bracha the warden? Just some influential piece of psychotic shit that acts as top dog? I might not have had any banal questions about who the woman who cleans the blood from the walls is when he invited query earlier on, but I sure as shit have some questions for Benny's tour of the funhouse now.

The lights flicker on, once again, above my head. The lights outside of the mad Yank's door spark and switch off. Surely somebody is taking the piss out of me here.

"Would you mind passing those back?" asks the stifled voice of Godwin behind the door. I don't know what else to do other than comply with his request, and I slide the papers back to him. "And the mirror?" There's this urge in me to smash the mirror, to crunch it underfoot until it's dust, but I don't do it. It's not my property. I smash it and there's a chance that I'll be up in court for destroying an inmate- A resident's property and infringing upon his human rights. I slide the mirror under the door an inch and it is snatched away with zeal.

"Thank you," he says, "now, kindly fuck off."

"Wait," I say.

[61]

"Hmm?"

"Who's Bracha?"

"If you don't know," he says, "then I can't tell you. *Benny* knows."

"But-"

SLAM.

The door at the end of the corridor opens. Benny.

"Kill him," says the voice behind the door, "before he kills you."

"Shut up."

"Huh?" Benny says through heavy breaths.

"Nothing," I say.

He seems happy with that.

"Okay. It looks like I can get one light working at a time. Not ideal. I'm sorry to be putting on you like this, especially on your first day."

"It's fine."

"How've they been?" he asks, looking pointedly at Godwin's door. I shrug.

"That good, eh?"

"So-so. They've-"

A wail from the next door interrupts me. Keith. Benny rolls his eyes. His sweating face reddens in the light above our heads, and he stomps over to the door. Punching it hard with the side of his fist.

"Shut the fuck up Keith! Don't make me come in there and burn your arse."

The wail quietens. A sobbing response from the room is barely intelligible.

"Yeah, I thought so," says Benny, "trying to fix these fucking lights and you're whining like a bitch."

He turns back to me. Smiles. Shrugs.

"I'm only kidding around," he whispers, "we're not allowed matches or anything up here," he whispers, "you don't smoke, do you?"

I make a face. I *do* smoke. He returns the look with another trademark eye-roll. He beckons me to the window at the end of the corridor. I follow, and watch him creak the archaic handles upright, before pushing the window open.

"Yeah, me too," he says, pulling a pack of cigarettes from his trouser pocket. In the glow of the moonlight his huge cock casts a bizarre shadow on the pale blue floor of the corridor. He hands me a cig and tugs a Zippo lighter from his tight trouser pocket. His double chinned face glimmers orange above the flame as he lights his smoke and then holds the lighter my way which I gratefully take advantage of. The nicotine doesn't take long to weave its goodness into my bloodstream and a woozy rush grips my brain.

"Don't tell anybody though, eh?" he grins. In this light his beard is three or four different colours. The chin and cheeks are brown, around the moustache it's more yellow, and around the sideburns it's a definite ginger. Everywhere else it's white. Something clicks.

"Have you always had a beard?" I ask. He shakes his head, no.

"No, only grew it recently, the wife asked me to, said she liked beards suddenly." His free hand comes up to rub against the growth on his face. Then he laughs. "Maybe her boyfriend has a beard, maybe she wants one at home too."

"No, I mean-"

I pause. He stops laughing. His joke obviously failed to hit the target.

"Huh?"

I shake my head.

"Nevermind."

We each smoke in a silence that's punctuated by screams from Keith. Each wail draws an impatient sigh from Benny.

"What's up with him?" I ask, blowing an arrow of smoke out into the cool air beyond the window.

Benny shakes his head.

"You don't wanna know," he says.

A Burning Passion

By Keith Nixon

I'M PUTTING the finishing touches to my latest work. This one is oil on canvas. I like oils because of the texture they deliver. Makes the visual rendering more lifelike. I drop the brush, ignore the splatter across the floor. Hold my head in my hands as the memories kick in, so (painful) my vision distorts. I can hear screams.

Eventually the convulsion passes.

I turn back to my easel.

"What's today's work?" she asks me. Always cold, always professional.

She's always there, my shrink. Hates being called that. No idea what she prefers. Don't care. The word had generated an outburst from her just the once, the single time the ice-hearted bitch had reacted. That was in the early days. Never get anything now, which is best for both of us. It affects the patient - which is me, by the way.

Because, as usual, I ignore her she's driven to stand over my shoulder, to see for herself what I'm up to. I feel her presence, flickering eyes taking in everything. There's a breath like a bull's snort. The temperature is up a notch, but perhaps it's just my imagination. It could be the guards playing with the temperature controls again, despite my repeated complaints.

"Very good," she says. I imagine her tongue flicking out, like a snake's, testing the air.

"Must you?"

"What?" my shrink asks, although she knows damn well what is, because we've discussed this desire of hers to invade my personal space many times previously in the years I've been incarcerated.
"Back up."
I'd swear she laughs, but I know that's my fucked up imagination. Her sense of humour withered and died with mine. She can't display anything. I'm not here for fun. I'm here for punishment. For retribution. For balance.
Nevertheless she does as I demand, retreats up against the wall, where we've agreed she must stay. No interference.
Another of my regular requests is to replace her but the hospital wouldn't comply. Said there wasn't anyone suitable.
Fine, I'd replied, but get rid of her. Anyone but her.
Who? they'd said.
I know it's a ploy. Designed to shake something out of me. But it won't work. I resist. Paint these days.
And write a bit too.

***

April 2nd

It's my birthday. Another year on. Friends, those I hadn't driven away, told me I should get back in the saddle. Whatever that means. Sounded dubious.
And I find it hard, meeting people. Even harder after the love of your life was taken in a meaningless accident.
I'd no desire to meet anyone. Ever again. But Jane wouldn't have it. Behind my back signed me up to an online dating agency. I only learnt about it when I received an email from an interested party.

"All the rage," said Jane, then told me to shut my mouth, which had flapped open like a hangman's trapdoor.

***

"Have you been keeping the diary as we discussed?" asks my shrink.
"No," I lie.
"Ok, good." She speaks with such certainty it's as if she can see into my heart, into my soul.
I slap some more oil onto canvas, build another layer of red onto the yellow, make it burn hotter.
I recline, stretch my spine, hear the tendons click as everything falls back into place. There's not much more I can add to the display for now. The flames are there, as are the screaming faces.
It's supposed to be therapeutic, but all it does is make me relive the nightmare.

***

April 3rd

Had a great night out, felt like I'd never stopped laughing. First time that had happened for... well, forever. Too long. Got so drunk I'd finally given into Jane's nagging to go out on the date her agency organised.
I've been back at work for a few months. Being an accountant at a medium sized company isn't a source of hilarity at the best of times. The finance department has its own office and very few visitors. Only other accountants seem to want to discuss fascinating stuff like cash flow ratios and net present values.

Now, sales and marketing the next space along, they seem to be a laugh a minute. I'm surprised any work ever occurs. Training? Even worse. There's one guy, a northerner, never shuts up. Said it was his job to talk. Talk shite in reality.
But I digress.
I agreed to the date.
Stupid mistake.

***

"Is that it?" she asks.
"What is it with all the questions?" I bite back, immediately kick myself.
"My job," she says. Probably pleased I've reacted.
I stand, retreat to my bed, lie down, keeping my eyes averted throughout. I shutter my vision.
No mattress, hard board. At first they'd kept replacing the mattress, but, once I'd burned it a couple of times, the guards gave up. They didn't want the hassle. It's my way of increasing the punishment. Self-inflicted. For killing everyone. A tiny price to pay.
I feel, more than hear her move again, glides on by. I fight down the anger. It's what she wants.
Because she knows not to do it. I've painted a rectangle on the cell floor. Dashed lines as a demarcation. Like the technical box football managers cannot stray out of during a match. It's where she's supposed to stay, but often doesn't. If I'm to be observed, let me have some control.
She's appraising my work, evaluating what it means. But it's simply a photo. A memory.

***

April 4th

The date. It went like a dream.
"Best just to get on with it," Jane had said. So I did.
She was as nervous as me. Turns out we work for the
same company, but different buildings. She's in R&D,
a boffin. Bright, very assured in her work, soft as
putty in her personal life, though.
Difficult divorce it seemed-aren't they always? I'd
replied. No desire to discuss it, so I didn't press.
We ate Italian. She laughed at my wine choice -
Lambrusco.
"No one drinks that anymore," she'd said.
"Very under rated," I'd replied.
The rest of the evening was a blur. Probably because I
drank too much. Nerves.
But I got her number. And a kiss. On both cheeks.
Very European.

***

"What are you trying to express?" she asks.
I click open my eyes. Stare at the bulb overhead. It's
behind toughened glass way up high, so it's hard to
reach. But not impossible. Plastic too. So nothing
sharp to slash my wrists with. Not that I want to die.
Too early.
I've managed to paint it red, much to their disgust.
Something else they've eventually given up on. Tried
to clean it off when I was out exercising, but I'd just
paint it again.
Of course it's red. What else could it be?
"Death," I reply. Click my eyes shut again and watch
the film playing in my head.

***

April 30th

It's a whirlwind. You hear about these things, but
never believe they'll happen to you. Romances that
blossom like spring flowers. Barren, cold earth one
day, glorious blooms the next.
We've seen each other constantly. She's stayed
around at my place. Met the kids. My son hated her,
no-one can replace his mother, of course. But my girl
doted on Susan. Her presents, a continual stream of
Disney DVDs probably helped.
But then the kids have been a mess since their father
left and their mother died. I'm just the stepdad, no
genetic relationship binds us. But I feel a powerful
responsibility. For the kids have no other family, my
wife was an orphan.
Jane wasn't so keen either, despite her earlier
conviction. Says she's heard stuff about Susan.
I don't care. Think I'll ask Susan to marry me soon.
Give the children a mother again...

***

I can hear her flipping through my art. The rattle of
frame against frame as one knocks into the other.
Oil is the latest medium. I've done watercolour, pen
and ink, charcoal. But none have the dramatics of oil.
It's the texture, see.
I turn my head away. Don't want to see her face, can't
see her face. It's too painful.
Instead I raise my arms, stare at the scars. For I have
them on the outside, as well as on my soul.
Livid, puckered, ever present. I pick at a scab. Make
the crimson flow.

***

May 16th

I can't fucking believe it. We're through. Over. Finito.
Asked her to marry me. Flashed the expensive ring.
She'd said no! Really lost her temper with me, said I'd
ruined everything.
I'm confused as hell. Ruined it how?
She won't return my calls. My daughter is missing
her, the boy and Jane don't. But for me light has
turned to dark once more.

***

"Look, you're bleeding again," she says.
I can feel her leaning over, vision boring into me. It's
definitely, I'm certain it's down to the guards. At her
behest though. But it won't work.
Keep my eyes closed, maybe she'll go away. Slither
back to her own space. Leave me mine.
"Cat got your tongue?" I know she likes that
reference.
"No." Not feline, a lizard. "You're making me
uncomfortable."
She apologises, but the expression lack sincerity.
Hovers over me a moment longer, just to
demonstrate I'm. It the boss. Retreats again.
Temperature drops a little. But I'm sweating, like I've
been leaning against a radiator on full blast.
Pop open my eyes. They're feeling dry, but I can't cry.
On the wall are flames.

***

[71]

May 23rd

The police have finally been. At last responded to my
repeated calls. But a stony faced female PC, called
Armitage, gave me a serious dressing down, rather
than the support I'd hoped for.
Told me to leave Susan alone. She ignored my
protests of innocence. That it was she harassing me.
Mud flinging accusations of seeing another woman.
I'm not. A case of not wanting me, but no-one else
being able to have me either, I think.
Armitage wouldn't or couldn't accept that I was the
one being harassed, rather than the harassee. Seems
it has to be the man, can never the woman.
She gave me a severe warning. Then left.

***

My cell. It's on fire. Flames are everywhere. On every
wall. Feet high, reaching as high to the ceiling as I can.
I feel her tracing the patterns out, brushing her claws
on the brickwork.
Sets my synapses off.

***

May 26th

So I took things into my own hands. Bought a
camcorder. Set it up in a bedroom, overlooking my
drive, the street beyond, the fence and the park
behind. Where she stands often, under a tree to
watch me.
Showed the footage to Armitage. I'm determined
she'll believe me.
But apparently it's not proper evidence, she said.

Eventually she agreed to talk to Susan, there was a slew of reluctance in her voice. But I'd threatened to go higher, see her bosses, speak to the press. Generated a tic under her eye. As she left Armitage suggested I should keep a diary.
First good idea she'd had.

***

June 1st

It did no good. Susan denied everything, even though I know it's her. PC Armitage told me again it was a lack of hard evidence. Slashed tyres, phone calls with no-one at the other end, smashed windows. Means nothing. It could be anyone. So I can't go around accusing people until there's a certainty of conviction. I told Armitage we can all make assumptions, asked her if she was a lesbian. It went rather quiet then...

***

"Why are you here?" she asks. More questions.
"You know why."
"Tell me anyway."
Anything to shut her up. "I killed people."
"Did you?"
I shrug. "They're dead."
"Atonement then."
"Yes. Every second of every day till it's my time."
"But it will never be enough."
"No."
How can it be?

***

August 9th

Today I wished I'd died.
The kids were home, couldn't stay at their friends any longer. Something woke me. A 6th sense. It was very late, or early depending on your perspective. The clock said 2.05am.
Checked on the kids. Both asleep in their beds, curled up.
I went downstairs, one step at a time. Listen after each minuscule descent. It was utterly silent.
In the kitchen I found the cat. Sprawled at a funny angle. As I bent down to take a closer look, felt a sharp blow at the back of my head.
Darkness.
When I awoke it was light. But not because of the sun. My house was alight. I tried to get up. But didn't get far because of the steel handcuffs that bound me to the fence. Ratcheted tight around my wrist.
"Don't worry!" she'd shouted, framed in the doorway, flames at her back. "They'll feel nothing."
I struggled to understand her. Too much to take in. Head hurt.
"It's not fair they suffer for your errors!"
She smiled at me, then closed the door.
Claws ripped out my guts right then. I pulled at the cuffs, tried to yank my arm off. But there was nothing I could do but watch my house burn. Flames licked upwards, blew out windows, turned everything to ash. It roared.
I was still screaming when the fire brigade and PC Armitage arrived.
They brought me here that day, and I've never been anywhere else since.

***

I feel a hot finger on my cheek.

"Observe me," she says.

"No." A whisper.

"See me!"

"No!"

But I can't help myself. Look up into her face. Susan's. She's on fire. Leans over to kiss me. Flames belch out of her mouth.

I scream.

Five

Benny lights another cigarette for each of us, before passing one to me. Keith screams again. Another lick of the flames from whoever.

"It's probably because he's ginger," says Benny, blowing smoke out as he says it.

"What do you mean?" I ask.

"Well, they can't handle the heat as well as most, can they?"

"I think that's just the sun," I say, "I'm sure we all deal with fire the same."

"I was kidding," he says.

"Oh."

He laughs as he takes another drag on his cigarette.

"You'll need a better sense of humour around here, mate," he says.

You need to be funnier, I don't say.

"I'll bear that in mind," I say, and take another drag. The nicotine influx has become the norm by now, and it's now the carcinogens that are working on my senses. The taste of the tar leaves a bad taste in my mouth, and I flick my second cig away, half finished. Benny seems unimpressed, but says nothing. Instead he changes the subject.

"I'm gonna need to go and carry on with these lights if we want to chill out later," he says. I nod with a half-smile and a roll of my eyes that mirrors that of the one he's been practising all night.

"Do I need to carry on here then, yeah?"

"Do you mind?"

Do I mind? Do I have a fucking choice, is a better question. I shrug. He pulls more joy from the cig, and flicks away the butt, before he closes the window. His hand wafts away the smoke as if it makes a difference. There's nobody of authority other than us around here, and the corridor stinks of smoke anyway, so even if there was it'd probably be a huge case of closing the door whilst we watch the horse galloping off into the horizon. A thought occurs from earlier, and I start to take my chance to ask a question but he speaks before I do.

"Okay, cheers. It shouldn't be too much longer," he says, pulling himself upright and straightening his trousers. As if he needs to. The fat, and that massive cock are doing the ironing for him.

"Who's Bracha?" I ask.

"I think I know what the problem is," he says, "I'll sort it," he says, "then we can order a curry or something."

"Is he the boss around here?" I ask.

"What kind of curry do you like?" he asks, "I prefer something hot, but I like it to have flavour," he says, "y'know?"

Benny neither answers my question, nor awaits a response to his own. He just slaps a hard hand onto my shoulder and walks away. The moonlight casts a pale blue glow against his big back as he wanders away from me. I look out onto the grounds of St. David's. My imagination invents yet another something skipping through the bushes and across the grass, and I turn to mention it to Benny but he's gone. The door to the stairs remains still. I shake my head, but it's not doing anything to fetch Benny back into the hall. The light above Keith's door flickers into being. The moth makes its way along the ceiling some more, and goes toes to toe with the radiance behind the plastic casing once again. This place is doing my head in.

I cough some fresh tarry phlegm from my throat, swallow it loudly, and then I let my gaze settle on the first door on my right. It's another grated door.

[77]

They always seem to hold the fruitiest of cakes in my short experience so far. Before I know what's happening I'm standing there before it. I let my eyes flicker to the name plate. On the slate it reads *Wilson, Mark*, but beneath, probably by the same hand the same prankster from Furchtenicht's door, probably Benny, it reads *Mary Magdalene.*

Fuck's sake, I don't say, as I knock a steady rhythm onto Wilson's door.

Mary Magdalene

By Mark Wilson

"HELLO? I'm here to fix the lights.
Can you get in the corner, please?" I press my ear up
against the door, listening for shuffling to confirm
that he's done as I asked. All I hear is a rhythmic
slurping, slap sound. I listen a little closer. The meaty
slurp sounds like it's coming from a distance away so
I slip my key in the door, turn and push gently,
keeping a firm hold of the handle, in case I have to
slam it closed again.

Peeking my face through the grate, I see
Wilson in the corner. More precisely, I see the back of
him. He's sitting in the corner like I asked, but I get
the distinct impression that he was already there
before I came knocking. He's not that tall, and only
lightly built but even from behind it's clear that he's
powerful. He has that wiry, coiled spring
musculature, I can see it in the movement of his
shoulder. I can see his body quite clearly as there's
nothing covering it.

His right arm is moving with some force,
repeatedly hammering away at something as he sits.
He's talking to himself, but I can't quite make out
what he's saying. It's not the accent, it's his voice, so
gentle. Like he's talking to a lover. He's facing the wall
to his right, staring at a photograph. I move a little
closer, just close enough to hear better and get a look
at the image. It's a tattered photo from some sort of
boarding school. There are about a hundred kids, half
a dozen nuns and maybe twenty priests, all standing

in rows posing for the camera. I peer in a little closer and start counting. Fourteen of the priests and two nuns have a very thick, very bold tick made with a red marker on their faces.

I cock my ear to the left and hold my breath. Wilson hasn't made a move, just that piston he has for a right arm pumping up and down in a decidedly masturbatory manner. *So long as he's happy.* I take another step closer, finally I can hear that gentle voice.

"Cotter, Docherty, McNally, O'Donnell, McGuire..." He lists surnames, maybe ten, maybe twenty and starts again, tugging at his cock with each name whispered. I've somehow forgotten why I'm here or the danger present and lean in for a closer look.

Wilson stands and turns quite gracefully as my foot scuffs the stone floor a little louder than intended. The cock-bashing hasn't stopped, or even slowed, it hasn't changed pace, I'm suddenly very grateful that it hasn't sped up. He tilts his head very slightly. His shaved head glints in the moonlight and his eyes widen as he takes me in. There are scars on his chest, low down just above the abdomen. They look nasty.

"Lalley, O'Malley, Foley.." His head straightens and the chanting stops, although the arm keeps perfect time.

"Are you fixing the lights or not," he asks, never missing a stroke. His voice is softer than any man's, he sounds like a woman, a pretty woman. I search for words, but my capacity to speak has been taken away by the sight of this very slight man with a cock like two cans of Red Bull stacked on end, wanking at me.

His arm starts to slow, so I start talking. "Yes, sorry Mr Wilson, if you could just stay in the corner, I'll.."

"What's your name?" He asks gently. His eyes are curious, but something else, there's excitement there, and maybe fear as well.

I tell him my name.

His face softened, and he tilts his head again, throwing me a seductive look.

"Are you a religious man?" he asks, with a giggle.

Involuntarily, my eyes dart to the faded image on the wall and back to his quickly. Not quick enough though, he saw it. His eyes narrow, all friendliness gone.

"My sister asked you a fuckin' question, cunt!" he roars at me in a booming baritone.

The change in him is staggering. The softness is gone, so has the curiosity. His whole posture has changed, all playfulness and grace has vanished and pure predatory aggression glares from him.

Fuck knows what the right answer to his question is but his arm has started pulling at that two-can cock with such ferocity that I'm genuinely frightened for its well-being despite the danger I'm in.

I blurt out, "No, I'm not. Used to be, but.."

"Shut the fuck up, ya dick." He spits at me.

I do. I watch him transform again in front of me. The face softens, the eyes widen and the body becomes a graceful swan in movement once again as *she* returns.

Something's changed in *her* though, *she's* no longer throwing me admiring, curious looks. She's looks friendly enough, and *her* wanking has returned to normal pace, but something's shifted.

She moves beside me to get a good look at my face. I use my peripheral vision to make sure that I have an egress.

"I'm sorry about my brother. He's a little overprotective," she says gently. "I'm glad you're not religious, I like the religious type, but Paul, my brother, does not."

"Okay," I sing, with false cheeriness as the lean man with the woman's demeanour and voice wanks serenely in my direction. "Best get on then. Would you mind going back to the corner, don't let me interrupt…" I nod down at her… his reddened cock.

"I'd like you to stay for a few minutes. I so rarely get to talk to anyone." Her face darkened a little, the threat of Paul behind her eyes. "Paul gets angry if I'm not happy. Let's talk, just for a little while." I nod and watch *her* walk back to *her* corner and resume *her* previous position, only this time *she's* facing me.

I sit a few metres away and ask. "So what's a nice girl like you doing here?"

Her face drops. "I'm not a nice girl," *she* says.

"I'm sorry," I blurt out, it was just a joke, y'know, cos that's what people say."

She nods, but I can tell that I hurt *her* feelings because *her* cock twitched at me in response.

"Why don't you tell me how you came to be here, you and your brother," I suggest. "if you don't mind, that is…." I suddenly feel ridiculous, but have to ask.

"What's your name?" I ask.

The wiry little, very scary man with the huge dick, blushes, he actually blushes and pauses his wankery for a second in surprise.

"Nobody ever asks me that, not in all my time here. They just call us both Wilson." *She* smiles with genuine warmth before resuming *her* stroking at a more leisurely pace than I'd seen *her* do so far.

"My name's Mary. Pleased to meet you."

"And you," I say with a ridiculous little bow that makes me feel stupid, but it makes *her* laugh and the cell lights up when *she* laughs.

"Would you like to hear about how I came here? *She* asks
I shrug, "Only if you're happy to tell me."
She gives me a little bow of her own, mirroring mine in a gentle mock, making me laugh. *Her* eyes dance with light and *she* drinks in my happiness as *she* starts to tell her story. I sit and stare into the face of the scariest, most beautiful man I've ever seen as he-she, as Paul-Mary speaks.

***

My sibling and I had been in St Margaret Mary's for around six months. We'd been to other schools, loads actually. We were good kids, but dad moved around a lot. Army officer. Came from money and gentry, couldn't be bothered being a parent after Mum died. It was an alright school and was close to Edinburgh city centre which was awesome for a couple of fourteen year olds with time to kill and no parents around.

On our first day, the head teacher, Father Connelly, introduced us to our peers at the house assembly. He made a big deal of us being twins, we were the first twins to attend St Mags'. Father Connelly was a lovely man, I really looked up to him, to all of the staff, to be honest. That's probably why I have a thing for the religious type, especially Catholics. Never works out though.

Paul played rugby, Mary studied hard. Friends were difficult to come by, most of the kids our age seemed withdrawn, sullen. We didn't particularly care, we had each other after all, but it would've been nice to have some more friends.

Eventually we were invited along to one of Fr Connelly's private dinners. He'd been telling us for

[83]

months how special being twins was. He really liked that about us.

Mary wore a very white dress, one that father Connelly had remarked on at an assembly some months before. Paul looked as scruffy as always, but at least he'd had a shower. When we entered Fr Connelly's quarters, a huge table filled the room. On it was a large white sheet, covering the food and around it sat sixteen of the school's priests and four nuns. I remember our eyes fixing on the sheet. Paul took Mary's hand and began to drag her back towards the oak doors we'd entered by, but Mary pulled free of his grasp. This was Mary's big night, and Paul wasn't going to spoil it.

I remember rushing to Fr Connelly and apologising. He smelled strongly of wine, they all looked a little drunk, even the nuns. Paul grabbed Mary from out of Fr Connelly's hands, she let him this time. The elderly priest we had so admired smiled at us as we backed up to the doors. Doors that had already been locked.

Paul rushed at Father Connelly and rugby tackled the head teacher to the floor, clattering the old man's head against a strong wooden chair leg as they fell. The room erupted, in laughter. Strong hands grabbed at Paul, grabbed at Mary also. Strong hands tore off our clothes and bound us and violated our bodies.

They passed us round. The tore our bodies as well as our clothes. They fucked the nuns, they pulled the sheet from the table and fucked each other with the implements of sex that lay there. They pushed them into us as well, those *toys*.

Hours passed I came and went. Some minutes passed torturously as years of pain and humiliation. Some hours passed in seconds of unconsciousness when I blacked out. *Mary, Mary Magdalene. Fuck Mary Magdalene,* they chanted as they passed us around.

      I woke many miles from St Mags on a rocky shore of the Firth of Forth. I'd been tied in a mail sack, along with my sibling. I'd freed my head and breathed. My sibling had not. It was a mercy. I climbed out of the sack and onto the smooth, cold pebbles of North Queensferry, a wretched creature. I kicked the body of my twin, still inside the sack back into the water and blew it a kiss.

      I didn't go back to Edinburgh, instead I went home to Dundee and emptied my father's safe at home. I went online with the black book full of passwords I found in his safe and emptied every one of his accounts too. The bastard deserved us for putting us in St Mags'.

      I disappeared. I got a new identity, I travelled, I grew up. I came back to Edinburgh, but I'd changed. I'd grown, become a man. A strong man, younger and more capable than the elderly, filthy men who'd violated Mary and Paul. The first one, I took whilst he crossed Charlotte Square. It was pathetic how old he had become. The hands I remembered clawing at my thighs and pants, were sparrow's claws, ineffectually pulling at my grip as I dragged the old cunt into the back of my van. I bestowed upon him every torture my sibling and I had suffered at his hands and the hands of his brethren.

      I went so much further with him than even they had with Paul and Mary. I cut his eyelids and placed him in a room full of mirrors to watch as I sliced and pierced and fucked and ripped and gouged every ounce of fucking pain I could drag from the evil bastard. I did things to that creature that some would

[85]

say makes me worse than all of them. It doesn't though, because he wasn't a child. That's the bare truth of it. He and his brothers of the cloth, men of God, betrayed children. I tortured and fucked an evil old man into a bloody puddle, then I hunted some of his fellow holy men. I still have some to find, to punish. For me and for my brother.

***

My eyes are stinging and I become aware that I hadn't blinked the entire time Wilson had been speaking. He's still sitting in Buddha position wanking away in the corner.

"Your brother?" I ask.

"Yes, Paul, my brother." *She* makes a sort of 'duh' face at me. Standing, *she* continues tugging on her cock and extends a hand for me.

"Thanks for listening. You should go now, Paul will be back soon. He doesn't like you much. Go."

I reach out and give the offered hand a little squeeze, similar to the one Benny had offered me earlier. As I let go my eyes go for a wander to Wilson's feet. They are small, maybe a size four or five. The legs are lean and strong but long and slender also. Whilst Wilson's torso is scarred the scars screamed a familiarity. I've seen scars like those on she wears on his-her chest somewhere else before. Maybe a TV show.

Wilson catches me scanning his body. That smile lights up the room again.

"You like it?" *She* asks. "I paid a fortune for it. Tits out and sewed up, vagina closed and this," She jerks that cock. "This I'm delighted with. Nice and big, plenty of damage done tae a hole wi' this big bastard, I can tell ye. Three piece titanium rod inside, hard whenever I want for however long I need it."

I gape at the scars.

"Only problem is that I'm a dry-shagger. They cannae give ye baws, well wee rubber wans, but not working ones full of spunk." *Her* eyes mist for a second as she loses herself in a rapey-reverie. "Och I'd have loved it if I could've had spunk tae splash over thae bastards," she says, wistfully.

Suddenly her face begins to darken once more and her voice deepens. Half way between Paul and Mary he-she roars. "Get fuckin' oot!"

She doesn't have to tell me twice. I rocket through the door and lock it shut behind me. Peering in through the little trap, I watch Mary kneel back into the corner and her back straighten. Paul's voice comes.

"Mary Magdalene. Mary Magdalene. Mary Magdalene. She's fuckin' coming fur ye, ya basturts."

Six

As the light above Keith's door blinks off, the one
above me sparks into being, and the temperature
drops cold. That kind of cold in the atmosphere that
you get when it's about to start thundering. When
you just *know* that a storm is brewing, no matter
whether you're inside with the radiators on full or
out there in a t-shirt, just about to get caught short
because it was gloriously sunny when you left the
house, and a coat would have simply been a
hindrance. It's that kind of cold. In the glimmering
radiance which falls around me from the only light in
the corridor that's working I can see a faint ghosting
of my breath, swirling and spilling from my mouth
and into the hall. Wilson, or *Paul,* or *Mary* continues
to thump their fist against an erect titanium cock. The
rhythmic slap of *wee rubber balls* against thighs. The
thing behind the door is all kinds of damaged.
Physically and mentally. Beyond redemption. The
tender look in its eyes when it was Mary, the kind of
look that you could fall in love with. The kind of look
that would throw you so far off track that by the time
you remembered yourself it would be too late. You'd
be having your throat ripped out by her violent alter-
ego as he fucked your arse until you were torn like a
lone ragdoll in the company of possessive twins. My
lungs involuntarily and suddenly demand a sharp
intake, as they remember that I haven't been
breathing since I left Wilson's room. My hand
searches for the wall to steady myself, and I take
another minute to compose.

      The moth – my only company on this bizarre
endeavour, since Benny continues to perform
genocide on my patience with his relentless
avoidance of all things insane – tip taps overhead.

Following the light. Following me. A wild goose chase on the path to clarity. To closure. If Benny could just keep the lights on, instead of somewhat inexplicably replacing one with another as I visit each inmate. Resident. I'd never noticed it before, but there's a blinking red light above the door to the stairs. A camera. Benny didn't say anything to me about CCTV. At least I don't think he did. Did he? I can't be sure. Either way, I certainly haven't been shown a monitor room. Is he in there now? Hilariously turning lights off and on to wind me up, in some ritualistic rite of passage for the new guy? Much the same as you might be sent out on your first day as a vocational apprentice at wherever, to find some tartan paint, only to return three hours later to mirth amongst your new workmates. This thought spikes in my mind and I'm abruptly self-conscious. I leave Wilson to its onanistic compulsion and approach the blinking light of the camera. It's not so state of the art that it has the ability to shift, so it simply stares right back at me as I look into its iris from the dark. My unmoving face off with whoever is, or isn't, watching me continues. Keith screams from the flames in his mind but I've grown accustomed to it. It doesn't frighten me anymore. I've been here less than two hours and already I feel like I've been here for years.

"Fuckin' dog!" bellows Furchtenicht as the light blinks once, twice, thrice, infinity. I continue to look up from the darkness.

"Lalley! O'Malley! Fuckin' Foley!" Paul roars from Wilson's mouth with each violent thump of their cock and still the light blinks once, twice, thrice, infinity.

"Kill *Benny*. Fuck him, before he fucks you," demands the calm voice of Godwin, beneath the shouts and screams, and *still* the light blinks once, twice, thrice infinity.

[89]

Then it happens. The camera's pupil dilates. There *is* somebody watching me. A quick dissolve transition edits my facial form from gormless stare to knowing grin. Without any prior warning my hand raises of its own accord, balled up into a fist, and my middle finger unfurls from the bud, alone. I'm on to them. I am *so* on to them. Whoever they are. I have a job to do.

        I spin on my heels and approach the sixth door in the hallway. It's a windowed affair. The kind of window I remember from school. The mottled and wobbly glass, fortified by the criss-cross of the thin wires. I stand before it and knock. Nothing. The slate beside the door says *Miles, Allen.* I remember Benny telling me that this is another one who demands to go by another name, but I don't remember what it was. Melchitt? I don't remember. I'm sure I'll find out soon enough. I knock again.

"Get in the corner," I say, keys out and door unlocked, "I'm here to fix the lights."

"Get-"

"If I could, I would, believe me," says the voice as I open the door. The voice belongs to a tall, slender man. He's laid upon a bed, one hand resting nonchalantly against his flat stomach, the other behind his head. At first it looks like he's supporting his neck, but as my eyes become accustomed to the dark it becomes apparent that the one hand is cuffed to the bed.

"You aren't here to fix the lights, are you?" he asks. He's well-spoken but with a definite northern edge, like a Yorkshireman with the rare ability to enunciate.

"I am, I'm-"

"I hate liars," he says, cutting me off, "liars do not deserve to breathe."

Still he doesn't move from the bed, or even try to. Just stares up at me from the thin mattress. Even in the dark I can make out unforgiving bruises on his cheeks and around his eyes. There's a black slice of an open wound across a recently broken nose. Several of his teeth are missing.

"Miles, I-"

"My name is Melluish. Vincent Melluish. You may call me Mr Melluish. If I hear the word *Miles* roll from your tongue again I will rip it out, do you hear?"

I nod.

"I'm going to give you one chance to redeem yourself," he says, and he gasps in pain from some internal injury as he twist his legs around as the mattress springs crunch harshly beneath him, his hand remains cuffed, thankfully, "would you like that one chance?"

I find myself nodding again. I daren't speak. His head drops, and for a brief moment it looks like he's dropped into a narcoleptic sleep, but then his face turns upward toward me and a malevolent smile breaks through the calm. Then he speaks.

"What's your favourite film?"

Clarity

By Allen Miles

A BURLY-LOOKING chap in orderly scrubs comes in and unhooks the CCTV camera. He looks at me and smirks, like he's got some sort of upper hand. I've been here for twenty-three days now and this will be the fourth time its happened. I don't care, to be honest. They think I'm insane. Nothing could be further from the truth. I'm what comic-book writers would call an avenging angel. In old testament times they'd call me a righteous man. I watch through the wired glass as dirty money changes hands between the security staff and some repulsive blob of humanity who is wearing an appalling fleece jacket and stone washed jeans ensemble. A guard with no academic qualifications unlocks the door to my cell and gestures him through with his baton. I lay down on my cot and stare at the ceiling as I hear him murmur to the fat boy,
"Ten minutes and that's it."
He pulls the door closed and locks it. Through the glass he smiles smugly at me and pockets the notes that this obese troll has paid him to allow him to have a small amount of time in my cell. I sit up and turn to receive my visitor. What a revolting specimen. Crew cut, beer gut, tattoos on his hands. The Northern Alpha Male. This man should have worn his finest suit to be in my presence. Still, one must be congenial.
"Good evening. My name is Vincent Melluish."
His teeth are already grinding, his eyes somewhere between tears and flames.
"Are you the one who killed my sister?"

"Erm, it's entirely possible. What was her name?"
"Sandra Fletcher."
"Fletcher.... Fletcher.... Ah, yes, the corpulent girl with the odour. Yes, I did kill her, very much so. But I assure you sir, I was entirely justified in taking her life, and she in no way suffered. She would have felt no more pain than a cow getting a nail shot into its head. Which is a remarkably apt metaphor, I'm sure you'll agree."

I don't think he quite understands what I said, but he heard confirmation that I terminated his sibling, which indeed I did. He comes flying at me with inked fists and steel toe-capped boots and within seconds he's broken my ribs, well, re-broken my ribs, knocked one of my teeth out and rived a fistful of hair from my scalp. I manage to block out the pain by revelling in the good work that I have done here, and I don't make a sound. Just as I begin to lose consciousness, as blows rain onto my head and gut, I force a peaceful, blissed-out expression onto my face. I am a perfectly serene little Zen garden in the bowels of this terrible place where they send murderers, rapists and psychopaths. I blackout as his sloping ape-like forehead connects powerfully with my cheekbone.

I'm not sure how much time I've lost. There are no days and nights here. There is no daylight or moonlight. I wake up in what they apparently call the medical bay. My ribs are taped and there are stitches above and below my right eye. My right hand is cuffed to the guard rail of the bed and my ankles are manacled together. How awfully undignified. A young man of south-east Asian origin approaches and politely asks me if I want something to eat. I decline with equal courtesy and ask his name, I've seen him on the ward before. They never tell the ancillary staff what our crimes are.

"My name is Rolando, Mr Melluish."

"Nice to meet you Rolando, you may call me Vincent."

"Thank you sir. I've been asked to tell you that you have an appointment with the psychiatrist in one hour. You'll be moved back to your... room."

"Thank you, Rolando."

He nods and walks away. He didn't want to say "cell", though he should have done. I dislike softening of the language intensely. He spoke to me with impeccable manners though, and will be spared when I get out of here. Two of the larger, security guard-type orderlies walk up to my bed and start barking instructions, military-style. I allow myself to be shoved about by these two apes, comfortable in the knowledge that they'll be dead once I escape. As they start unfastening my shackles when I'm back in my cell I look deeply into their eyes as I ask how their wives and/or children are. It has the intended effect and I can see that it puts the fear of God into them as they genuinely believe all the propaganda that they've been fed about me. They honestly think I'm a psychopath, the same as the rest of the social inadequates that they deal with in here. They leave me laid on my cot, my right wrist chained to a heavy steel ring attached to the wall, as it has been since I arrived here.

After twenty minutes or so, I hear high heels clip-clop their way down the corridor, and a tall, slender and bespectacled woman in a mid-priced suit carrying a briefcase is ushered into my cell. She sits down behind the high school desk that serves as my dining table and arranges papers on the scratched wooden surface. I haven't acknowledged her presence and I remain horizontal on my bunk.

"Good afternoon Vincent, I'm Dr Emily Lewis, your new psychiatric consultant. How are you today?"

For crying out loud...

"Dr Lewis, I neither gave you permission to sit nor address me by my first name. Kindly show some decorum in the future. Now, I was under the impression I was to be under the analysis of Dr Campling."

She looks completely affronted, which is exactly what I hoped for. She can pay me some respect from now on. She looks at me over the top of her spiky-framed glasses.

"Dr Campling decided she didn't want to continue with your case."

"Yes, I expected that would happen; she was a hopeless amateur, broke down and started weeping halfway through our last meeting. I'm amazed that these people who are so clearly out of their depth attain such positions."

"Well, I've taken over your case now. I hope we can work together. Now, I'd like to ask you a few questions if I may."

I fancy a fag. I know she's got some, I can smell it on her.

"Before we go any further, Dr Lewis, I'd like a cigarette."

"You're not allowed to smoke in here, Mr Melluish."

She gets a point for addressing me correctly, but I want a fag. With a jab of pain in my ribs, I swing myself into a sitting position and look at her. Her facial expression is one that is controlling her fear, but not concealing it. I smile and drop my gaze to the floor.

"If I don't get a cigarette, Dr Lewis, then I don't speak a single word to you."

She takes a packet of Lamberts from the inside pocket of her jacket and throws one into my lap. I put it to my lips and stare at her. A cheap plastic lighter lands on my bunk and I set fire to the carcinogens without ever taking my eyes away from hers. I hold the fag in my left hand because the chain on my right wrist doesn't reach my mouth.

She scrutinizes my face, obviously regarding the embroidery around my eye.

"What happened to...?"

"My face? The man who let you in here; his name is Gary. You should ask him. He'll tell you I fell down some stairs."

"Is that what happened?"

"Of course, Dr Lewis."

She neither believes me or cares what really happened and dismisses this section of our discourse with a petulant raise of the eyebrows. This woman has a clear agenda here.

"Can we talk about Miss Fletcher?"

I blow out a huge, luxurious cloud of midnight blue smoke and lay back down on my two inch mattress. I feel serene, and I'm willing to converse with this woman.

"Yes, by all means."

"You've admitted that you killed her?"

"Yes, of course. In a very profound sense."

I don't turn my head to look at her but I can sense that she's appalled.

"Why did think you had the right to kill this woman? How, as a human being, can you justify what you did?"

She's trying to remain professional here, but her own feelings are coming to the fore.

"Had you ever seen this woman, Dr Lewis?"

"Well, no. Of course not. Why would I have done?"

"If you had have done, you'd at least have some inkling of why I terminated her. She was a horrific example of this country's decline. A revolting, obese portrait of ignorance and sloth. She contributed nothing but offense to my senses, and when I first saw her it was all I could do to stop myself from vomiting. Good heavens, it took some effort. I assure you, Dr Lewis, it is better all round that I removed her from this life."

As she chews on the end of her biro, her face tenses, as if she is struggling to maintain her clinical demeanour. Outrage, whether forced or not, is not far below the surface here. She measures the tone of her voice in her head and replies.

"Mr Melluish, do you think it's okay to murder people because you object to their appearance?"

"Oh come now, Dr Lewis, the word "murder" is dreadfully coarse, and her appearance was only a fraction of the reason she had to be taken out."

"But you *did* murder her. And since you mentioned it, what was the rest of your motive?"

"You're trying to make me sound like a common criminal here, Dr Lewis. Kindly stop that."

"Why did you kill her, Mr Melluish?"

"I had stopped in the supermarket on my way to work. I was running late due to an imbecile having double-parked on the duel-carriageway and causing a huge traffic jam. I selected a sandwich and a bottle of fruit juice for my lunch and made my way to the self-serve check-out. As I approached it our friend Sandra waddled in front of me and proceeded to put an entire trolley-full of groceries through the self-serve facility! I couldn't believe what I was seeing. There were signs that clearly stated it was for hand-baskets only. Such ignorance, Dr Lewis! Such selfishness! How, and indeed why, Dr Lewis, are people like that allowed to be part of our society? I returned my goods to the shelf and followed her to her car. As she was loading her boot with her junk food I shot her in the back of the head. My gun was silenced and I made sure no children could have seen. She didn't feel a thing. I must stress doctor, that my motive wasn't borne of evil or hatred, I just decided that it would be better all-round if she didn't exist. It was a functional and clinical termination."

Her lips remain taut and silent, and her eyes take on the look of a child that is watching a cheetah kill a baby gazelle on a wildlife documentary as her parents explain that it's awful to watch, but simply the way of nature. She haphazardly thrusts her hand into her suit for a cigarette of her own, and as she irritably wrestles the pack from her pocket, a slip of paper flies out with it. In her haste she doesn't notice it fall to the floor. She lights her cigarette with a shaking hand and after the initial drag she seems to relax ever-so-slightly. She takes a deep second suck and blows it out through her nostrils. She looks at me and it almost seems like she grits her teeth before she speaks.

"What about the bin man? Why did you kill him?"

She's really cheapening my project here with her vulgar choice of words. She's also letting her profession down terribly. I doubt whether she is a psychiatrist at all.

"Dr Lewis, would you please stop using words like 'kill' and 'murder'? Such derogatory terms are not befitting of my work."

"You see taking people's lives as your work?"

"Absolutely. Now, let me tell you about the bin man, as you called him."

"Please do."

"Yes, well, as we are encouraged to do these days, I diligently recycle, or at least I did before my incarceration. I try to do my bit for the environment, as we all should. And one morning I was leaving for work, having put my blue bin outside, only to find that the luminously-clad primate who was supposed to empty my bin was refusing to do so. I politely queried his decision, and he said, and I quote 'Can't take polystyrene.' Now, I wasn't aware of this and I offered to remove the offending packaging from the bin but he said, and again I quote 'Too late, I've seen it now.' This brazenly deliberate attempt to be uncooperative astounded me, Dr Lewis, and although I engaged this Neanderthal in an utterly banal discourse for some time he still pointedly spurned my requests, and eventually, my demands to take my recyclable waste. This personage had the most miniscule amount of power, the slightest authority, and he was going to use it. What a dreadful situation. I had spent my own time dividing my refuse for the good of mankind, and this silly little man felt the need to make himself feel bigger by refusing to do his job on the basis of a tiny triviality. What a waste of a human body."

She hasn't noticed the slip that fell out of her pocket. I discreetly glance at it where it has landed under her chair as she looks for somewhere to dot her fag and eventually just rests it on the edge of the desk.

"So you murdered him because he wouldn't take your blue bin?"

"Once again you have made my work seem frivolous Dr Lewis. But yes, I called in absent and spent the day tracing his wagon to the depot he worked at. Once again I shot him in his car with a silencer. Clean, quick, painless. I simply removed someone who was too unpleasant to live."

"He had children, Mr Melluish, and a wife. Do you think it's okay to rob a family of its father?"

[99]

I take a second to articulate my response, whilst my analyst struggles with the realisation that she is woefully out of her depth here.

"I have two answers for you Dr Lewis. Either he and his wife were of similar personality, and had already foisted their horrific world views on their children, in which case they are beyond redemption; or the rest of his family hated him and will be better off without him. Either way, the termination will not affect the family."

I look around at my cell. The walls are slathered in thick, cheap, sickly grey emulsion and the floor is bare concrete. There is a wired glass window in the heavy steel door through which can be seen the main security point for this section of the asylum. I'm pretty certain I'm below ground level. I haven't breathed fresh air since the day I was incarcerated. It's always one of the same two men on that desk. They swap shifts at eight in the evening. I've been studying their routines and movements obsessively. Not only theirs, but those of the catering staff, the medical staff and the clinical professionals, such as our Dr Lewis here, all cross-referenced with my own exercise time and visits to the showers and such.

Dr Lewis is chewing at her lips. I suspect when she leaves me today she will ask to be taken off my case. A request that I would personally support, given the opportunity. She has been disrespectful and is clearly not up to interviewing me. She is scribbling in a note pad which I actually quite admire; the previous two had brought laptops in here with them.

She addresses me without looking up from her notes. "Tell me about your neighbour."

I raise my eyebrows and look at her patronisingly whilst making a gesture with my unchained hand which signifies that there is a word missing from her sentence. She takes a controlled and measured breath, takes her glasses off and rubs her eyes.

"Tell me about your neighbour, *please*."

Comfortable in the knowledge that I have broken this woman, I proceed to tell her about the termination of Shelton Hatfield, 27, unemployed.

"Ah yes, a moron of the highest order. A drain on the state. All he ever seemed to do was lay on his couch and smoke cannabis."

"You're anti-drugs, Mr Melluish?"

"No not at all, I don't object to people taking drugs in any way. What I do object to is people talking to me when they're on drugs, particularly cannabis. For example this chap, Mr Hatfield, enjoyed a most charmed upbringing, by all accounts. He grew up in Harrogate, and his father, a consultant gynaecologist, paid his way through university, where he laboured to a second class degree in something completely worthless like Latin or fine art. Yet for as long as I've known him he would wander out into his front yard whenever he saw me having a cigarette and start extolling the virtues of Jamaican reggae music. He used to tell me how he identified with it. In his words it "spoke to him". Isn't that amazing? This man, who had never known hardship in his whole life, who had been raised in relative luxury and never sought out employment because he had never needed to, found a spiritual connection with a music borne from abject poverty, gang warfare, gun crime and political oppression. What a deluded fool, Dr Lewis. What a disingenuous parasite of a man."

My analyst says nothing. She just looks at me with what I assume she thinks is a cold stare. I continue.

"He always used to play his music at the most obscene volume, and at the most anti-social of hours. He had a constant flow of similarly idiotic visitors

[101]

coming and going at all hours of the night, clattering and banging about, utterly oblivious to the fact that they were causing an ungodly cacophony and stopping me from sleeping."

I notice the tiniest pinprick of empathy in Dr Lewis's facial expression. The mauve circles under her eyes that she's attempted to cover with her make-up suggest that she too suffers from lack of sleep.

"He had a positively ghastly taste in music, too. As well as the reggae he frequently blasted through my wall there was also stuff like The Grateful Dead and The Eagles and also a lot of what I believe was termed stoner-rock, atrocious music that shouldn't be permitted. I used to be able to tolerate it though, Dr Lewis, because if I banged on the wall he generally turned it off. On the night I terminated him, though, he piqued my ire in the most reprehensible manner possible."

Dr Lewis forces an indifferent pout to her lips, unsuccessfully trying to mask the apprehension she's feeling.

"And how did he do that, Mr Melluish?"

"It was about midnight and I'd got in from my shift about an hour previously, I had my evening meal and sat down to read for a little while before retiring for the night. As ever, the music was coming through the wall but I didn't mind so much as I had donned my earplugs as I always do when I read. When it got to about quarter past, I noticed the volume of the music increased, and our man Shelton, without the slightest consideration for the good of civilisation, had decided to listen to the band "Queen".

Dr Lewis's brow furrows so intensely that it looks like you could fall into the grooves on her forehead and her mouth has dropped open long before she starts talking. I stick my tongue through the gap where my left incisor used to be.

"Are you seriously about to tell me you murdered this man because he liked listening to Queen?"

"Yes, absolutely. Well, not only that severe aberration in taste, but the fact he felt the need to foist it on his neighbours. I tried banging on the wall several times to no avail, so after I got to the point where I simply could not abide that ludicrous row anymore I went and knocked on his front door. There was no reply and the music continued. After a few more minutes of knocking I tried the door and entered his house. He was there on his couch, a take away spilled all over himself, empty beer bottles and over-flowing ash-trays everywhere, so narcotized he could barely move. It was a scene of the most wanton self-indulgence, an outrageous way to live, especially at the expense of the tax-payer. He noticed me even though he could barely open his eyes, and a pathetic, helpless smile formed across his lips. He raised his hand a few inches and tried to wave but it seemed to exhaust him. If I'm honest, Dr Lewis, I started to feel a bit sorry for him and I was about to call an ambulance, but then..."

I sigh and roll my eyes for dramatic effect. Dr Lewis sits forward in her chair and actually seems caught up in the story rather than trying to evaluate me.

"And then what?"

"At that moment Bohemian Rhapsody came on. Have you ever heard that song, Dr Lewis? I absolutely loathe it. Hailed by all as a classic when in actual fact it is six minutes of nonsense. My sympathy for Shelton was replaced by contempt and I shot him between the eyes as his stupid, sloppy mouth kept trying to smile. Again, I must re-iterate, that it was painless, clean and clinical."

Dr Lewis has now gone from being professionally fascinated to being personally mentally-assaulted. I'm pretty sure she wants out of here now, but she will have been told to ask about all four of my terminations. The one that, much to my regret, lead to my arrest. Silence hangs in the air and after a minute or so she's still sat there looking like a starving dog so I might as well take the lead here.
"Presumably you'll want to know about the most recent one as well, Dr Lewis?"
She fumbles around and lights another cigarette. She looks at me but doesn't make eye-contact.
"Yes I do, Mr Melluish. Tell me about the man in the penthouse."
"The man in the penthouse, Dr Lewis, was known to me only as Imnez. I met him for the first time about three months ago, when I'd been getting threatened at work by unsavoury types trying to collect on forged prescriptions. A friend of a friend put me in contact with him, and told me what services he could provide."
"And he sold you your gun?"
"Indeed he did."
"You killed him three weeks later. Why?"
"Because he was an arms dealer."
Dr Lewis looks completely incredulous, and raises her voice for the first time.
"But *you* bought a gun off him!"
As ever, I am the reflecting pool of calm.
"Yes that is correct, Dr Lewis, but I am a man of intellect and virtue. Imnez was selling guns to eighteen year olds who referred to themselves as gangsters, to petty thieves and drug dealers, to anyone, regardless of acumen, who would pay the requisite price. I had to stop that process."
"By shooting him yourself?"

She is screeching now. She's lost her professional facade and she's lost control. I've broken her. She won't be back again.

"Yes. I shot him with the very gun he sold me. Once again, quick, clinical, precise. He was an enormous man though, I shot him three times to be on the safe side. It is to my intense regret that I hadn't thought of the possibility that the CID may have been watching his apartment. I was arrested when I alighted from the lift in the building's lobby and a little while later I found myself here."

The cigarette protruding from Dr Lewis's fingers has a good inch of ash on it, which falls onto the desk as she jerks herself out of her reverential trance. She shuffles her papers and tries to look like a qualified psychiatrist, whatever they look like.

"Mr Melluish..."

"Please Dr Lewis, call me Vincent, there's no need to be so formal."

She drops her head, removes her glasses and rubs the bridge of her nose with her index finger and thumb. The classic sign of someone who is mentally spent. She looks up at me, again without making eye-contact, and almost seems haunted in some way, her eyes wide and pink. She inhales deeply before speaking.

"Vincent, you freely admit to these terrible crimes, and you show not even the slightest hint of remorse. You seem to view these murders, these killings that you have committed, as no more than everyday occurrences, no more serious than crossing a road or posting a letter. You don't seem to realise that this is not how society operates. I have never met a human being with such utter distain for his fellow man. It is my duty as a professional to report back to the courts that you are a severe danger to those around you and should be kept in solitary confinement for the rest of your life. You are without question sociopathic and almost certainly insane. In all my career, you are instantly the most mentally deranged person I have ever met."

She looks like she's about to burst into tears, her amateurish analysis having provided some sort of catharsis for her, but she's not getting the last word here. I stand up, and she recoils, even though the clank of the handcuff chain against the steel ring on the wall reassures her that I can't get within ten feet of her. I stare at her and make my eyes boar into hers. I hold her gaze for the first time and she doesn't look away.

" You may think I'm insane for what I did, Dr Lewis, but all I did was to painlessly end the lives of people who were too unpleasant or stupid to exist. Last week, a pregnant woman in Pakistan was stoned to death in front of cheering crowds because she married someone who worshipped a different invisible man in the sky to her family. Yet a few years ago a wealthy couple drank and socialised as their infant daughter was abducted whilst alone in a foreign country, and they were made martyrs and millionaires by the idiotic general public who bought into their lies. Stem cell researchers have studies which suggest that they could find a cure for cancer within five years, but they can't get public funding because the Catholic church have vetoed it. The Catholic church which has protected clergymen who have sexually abused those that trust them for hundreds of years. These things are the real insanities Dr Lewis, and they happen every single day in full public view and no-one bats an eyelid. I may have terminated four lives, but given the time and resources I would have done thousands, tens of thousands possibly. The fact that I am no longer willing to witness such ignorance and atrocity all the time doesn't make me insane, it makes me honest. And although it may make you feel terribly uncomfortable, there is a tiny, tiny part of you that wishes that you had the will and clarity of vision that I have. You can write up your little report there and go home and watch your soap operas and go out drinking and go to the gym, whatever, but on the day you die you'll realise that your life's work meant absolutely nothing. Mine will mean everything."

I take in the look of glassy-eyed mesmerisation on her face, and slowly close my eyes and sit back down. She collects her papers together, then without glancing back at me steps briskly to the door and hammers on it frantically. The guard lets her out and looks at me with the standard forced disgust. Once the door is shut I stretch out my leg and with the toe of my boot I'm able to slide the stray piece of paper from her handbag back over to my cot. It is a delivery invoice from Amazon for a DVD box set of Sex In The City. It has her home address on it.

I will decide over the next twenty-four hours whether Emily Lewis of 16 Bellfield Court will survive, (her choice of viewing material will weigh heavily against her) as tomorrow night the fatter of the two security guards, Gary, will have his weekly adulterous tryst in the cleaning cupboard with the girl who brings the laundry round and my escape plan will be put into operation.

My work will continue...

Seven

"Interesting," he says, after I reveal my favourite film, "I did not expect that. Usually the hired help around here are so terminally bland. The other guard, Gary, for example, he enjoys the music of Coldplay. He sings those rancid *tunes* to irritate me. Tell me, did you think it was better than the book?"

The man seems to want to get into something of a pop culture conversation, and I don't trust myself not to fall into a trap, but without a further thought I feel my mouth opening, and the words come spilling out like the remains of last night's vindaloo from a particularly hungover arsehole.

"I enjoyed them both in different ways," I say, "the film was less open to interpretation, but it was still a brilliant adaptation. It wouldn't be my favourite film if it weren't would it?"

Miles tilts his head just slightly as he looks at me, an intrigued expression on his face.

"What's your favourite music?" he asks.

"I thought you said I had one chance at redemption?" I say suspiciously. He rubs his chin with his free hand as he laughs.

"I suppose I did say that, and I do hate liars," he concedes, "but indulge me all the same, wouldn't you? I do so hate it when the only conversation I can get out of anybody is all about why I killed *her*, or why his children will miss him since I shot *him*, you know?"

I sigh, well aware that I'm walking a fine line. I shouldn't be engaging them like this. Miles frowns at my exhalation.

"Oh, I'm sorry for pining a little intelligent conversation Mr Sighsworth. Gary does have you on a tight lead doesn't he? Do you have better places to be?"

I sigh again, a little more impatiently this time, and I roll my eyes. I should have indulged him all along. Just for some fucking peace.

"Okay, I'm into- Wait. Who the fuck is Gary?"

Miles' face cracks into a satisfied grin, and his legs spin back onto his mattress, that same pained crunch of the springs, and he settles down, his free hand comes back to rest on his gut.

"It would appear I've said too much," he smiles, "I won't kill you, by the way, a little consolation for you, eh?"

"Seriously," I say, "Who's Gary?"

Miles closes his eyes as he shifts around on the bed, trying to find a comfortable spot. Says nothing.

"Is he Bracha?" I ask.

Miles hums *Lux Aeterna,* the orchestral theme tune of Requiem for a Dream. The film I told him was my favourite.

"Does Gary work with Benny?"

His free hand comes up to conduct the invisible orchestra as he builds up to a crescendo.

"Answer me! For fuck's sake!"

A door slams. Benny. I look down upon the musical fruitcake.

"This isn't over, *Allen.*"

His performance stops immediately. He bolts upright until the short chain of his cuff halts him, and he eyeballs me venomously.

"For that, you die tonight."

I exit the cell and smash the door closed. Before I know it I'm bounding down the stairs two at a time. Did I lock that door? It doesn't matter. He's chained up. I slip back into the ground floor corridor. The therapy rooms pass me by one after the other.

Bleeding therapy, intimidation therapy, electrical therapy, medicinal therapy, hypno-regression therapy, alternate therapy. The scratches on the door frame. They're from finger nails. They're from men who did not want to enter those rooms. They're from the inmates here. Not residents.

I round the corner quickly, and come crashing face to face into Benny. He stands firm and I bounce from him, onto the floor. My torch, once again goes skittering across the hallway floor.

"Alright?" he asks, an amused look in his eyes as he pulls me up from the deck, "you look like you've seen a ghost."

"Who's Gary?" I ask, my fists clenching and unclenching. He looks down to them, and rolls his eyes.

"You've seen Vincent, eh?"

"Allen, yeah."

"That's what he calls me," he says, "it's like a game we play."

"A game?"

"Yeah. It started a while back. He only answers to Vincent Melluish," he says, "so I started only answering to Gary," he says, "just to wind him up. In the end it just stuck."

None of us says anything after that. I'm still catching my breath, and I let his explanation work its way into my logic filters. I take the time to check his features. Is he lying? I don't know. It does seem like a plausible excuse. In *this* place of all places, that seems like a very plausible explanation.

"Look, I think I've got the lights fixed," he says.

His eyes remain on mine.

"I need you to go up and check," he says.

His beard is gone.

"What happened to your beard?" I ask.

"I just need you to get to the top of the stairs, and shout down if they're on, that's all."
No. I won't do it. The fat lump has ignored my questions all fucking night. If he wants any more help out of me then he can start fucking answering them.
"No, listen to me, Benny," I say, doing my best to stop from raising my voice, "you had a beard upstairs," I say, "something's not right. Who the fuck are you?"
The echo of a door slamming somewhere above us ricochets from every greasy surface in the place.
Benny looks at me, unnerved.
"You locked Vincent's door, right?"
I nod.
"Yes. I did. I think."
"You think? Aw, fuck."
Benny turns on his heels and leaves me alone.
"Wait!" I call out, but he's gone. I rapidly step after him, trying to keep up with him but for a big guy he can shift. By the time I reach the corner of the hallway he's gone. The brown sign from earlier. It reads *Confusion Therapy.* I shout his name. Nothing. I can't stay here anymore. I can't do it. The place is breaking me. I let Benny run off to wherever and I head back to the staff room. I'm not doing this anymore. Fuck my bills. Fuck my rent. Fuck everything. I'd rather be unemployed than have another minute here.

       The door to the staff room swings open, and he's there. Benny. Fat, annoying, bearded Benny.
"Hey, you're here, I managed to fix the lights," he says, "it was just a faulty switch. Emergency over," he smiles.
"What?" I ask incredulously, "What the fuck is happening?"

"What do you mean?" he asks, pulling a beer from the staff room fridge. The buzzing of the bulb overhead scratches at my eardrum. It makes my eyes hurt.

"You just went upstairs. You didn't have a beard. You. *Who the fuck are you?*"

Benny sighs.

"I'm Gary," he says, "Benny's brother," he says "Benny's twin brother."

"What the fuck?"

"I don't work here," he says, "I just help out."

The Twin Towers

By Ryan Bracha

BENNY AND GARY are identical twins. Except that Gary has a beard. All their lives they were bundled together. A team. A package. Double trouble. They didn't used to be called Benny and Gary. They used to be called something else.

When they were twelve, they took up boxing. They would show up together at the local gym, identical bags slung over each shoulder. They wore identical blue shorts, with tight white vests, and they wore identical gloves. They both stood at almost six feet tall even at that early age. The trainer at the gym, Jackie McVeigh called them *The Twin Towers,* and he coached the boys for years. Had every intention of raising them through the ranks together, a formidable duo that would carry the McVeigh name into the big time.

The thing was, Gary wasn't quite as naturally talented as his brother. He would only ever reach the levels of *Club Fighter,* never to be a true contender, simply a journeyman who'd take his fair share of beatings and walk away with the loser's pot. Where Benny was the real ability who would likely get his shot the world stage, Gary would probably nurse broken cheeks for months before he could climb back into the ring and take another beating.

This wasn't a major concern for Gary, he could take a punch, that's what he was good at, but Jackie McVeigh, he had other ideas. He had his dream of two championship fighters. The Twin Towers. Once upon a time, he took the boys to one side, and he put something to them. An idea. Jackie McVeigh suggested that Benny fight for the both of them. Gary would show up to weigh-in. Gary would spout shit to the local press about his opponent, and then Gary would head to his dressing room. Once he had disappeared from sight, his brother would reappear, and fight, and win, in his name. Then a few weeks later, Benny would fight under his own name, and the pair of them would be launched into the world of professional boxing.

Benny liked this idea. He loved it, in fact. Gary wasn't so sure. He was a man who liked to earn his own recognition, even if it meant losing. He was a man of pride, and honour. After so long, after all of the needling and cajoling from his twin brother and Jackie McVeigh, Gary eventually relented. He'd let them do what they wanted. They would go ahead with Jackie's plan.

Months passed, and Benny fought and won as both himself, and his brother. Took local belts as their own. No amateur title in Yorkshire didn't belong to the brothers. They were celebrated county champions in the local community. They even opened a branch of Jack Fulton in their village. Their parents were so proud. At family get-togethers they would be wheeled out and forced to spar with one another for the purposes of entertainment. In the blind enjoyment and pride of having two contenders sprout from his loins, the father never ever noticed that Gary's southpaw stance was what set them apart. Nobody ever noticed, and if they *did* notice, then they didn't ever mention it.

Then, one night, sometime in mid-September, the Twin Towers fell from grace.

Gary had been lined up to fight a bloke from Leeds. They went through the rigmarole of weigh-in and banter, and Benny was set emerge to take Gary's place in the ring. Only, Jackie McVeigh didn't emerge with him. Jackie McVeigh didn't emerge from anywhere ever again.

In the build-up to the fight, Gary had approached his trainer. He didn't enjoy what was happening. He couldn't stand by anymore and watch his brother do all of the work. He felt like a fake. It wasn't right. Jackie had told him to keep his mouth shut. Jackie said that they'd all go down for fraud. Jackie asked him if that was what he wanted. Jackie didn't listen. He had grabbed a hold of Gary's shoulders, shook him hard. Slapped his face and called him a stupid cunt. Told him to keep his stupid cunt mouth shut if he knew what was good for him. Told him he was a loser. Called him a failure. Said his brother would always be the achiever between them. So Gary took his trainer, and he showed him exactly how much power he had in his fist. He showed him exactly what he'd got in his locker. Gary didn't stop punching his trainer's face until his own fist was as broken as the skull of Jackie McVeigh. Even then he had to tug hard to get his smashed paw from the hole he'd beaten into that old face. Then he sat down. Gasping for breath. Looked down at the broken corpse of the man he'd killed. Then a scream. The ring girl had come to check on them. To see if they were okay. They weren't okay, far from it.

In the melee that ensued, Gary and his brother Benny disappeared for good. Benny couldn't stand by and watch his brother go down for his crime. They were brothers. Twins. No bond was greater than that of twins. So they left town, never to return. Left their parents to pick up the pieces. To answer the questions of the police. To accept the violent repercussions that would follow from Jackie

McVeigh's sons. The Gary and Benny of old disappeared. They let their bodies go to shit. The firm muscle in their honed bodies turned to sloppy fat. They started smoking, and drinking, and eating in excess. They lived their lives on the run. They took a job as one person at St. David's Asylum for the Criminally Insane. Two people, living their lives as one person. Much the same as half of the lunatics that lived there appeared to do. It seemed like a good idea at the time.

Every night, Benny and Gary will sit together in the security office of St. David's Asylum for the Criminally Insane, eating pizza, and drinking beer. They will take their turns to patrol the halls, calming down the inmates, and will in no way abuse their power. That's not what they do. They definitely do *not* abuse their power. No matter what anybody in here tells you, they are professionals.

Sometimes, though. Sometimes the agency sends somebody new. Then, and only then, do they let the mask slip just slightly. Then, and only then, do they get just a little territorial. Then, and only then, do start to act just a little out of character.

Eight

"Twins?" I ask. Gary nods.

"Mmhmm," he says, "Benny's older by fifteen minutes," he says, "and forty eight seconds."

After the night I've had, I'm close to admitting that I'm relieved that these two fuckwits have been messing with my head. I *knew* something wasn't right.

"I could get him sacked, you know that?" I say, my threat as empty as Gary's bearded head. Which is now shaking.

"Yeah, but you won't," he says.

"What makes you so sure?"

"Well, for one, there's two of us, and we'll just make sure you keep quiet."

"Okay?"

"And for two, we don't even exist."

"What?"

"You heard."

"What do you mean?"

"You're undergoing confusion therapy right now, you aren't here. We aren't here. You're a resident. You'll wake up before long and they'll drag you kicking and screaming back to your room."

Now I'm shaking my head, and laughing derisively. I'm a resident? I've never heard so much bullshit in all my life.

"You're fucking tapped mate," I say, jabbing a finger into the side of my skull, "are you sure *you're* not the *resident*?"

"Go and ask Benny if you don't believe me, he's upstairs sorting your mess out."

I'm out of the door and flying up the stinking sweaty corridor as fast as my legs will take me. From behind me I hear Gary's booming laughter. From above me I hear screaming. Fucking *Keith.* My steps feel heavy. I sluggishly drag myself up the stairs. At first it's two at a time and then it's one. The door to the first floor swings open before me and it's then that I see it. Allen Miles' door wide open. I didn't lock it. *Fuck's sake.* There's that scream again but it's not Keith. It's coming from Miles' room. I approach the open door. Inside it Miles, or Vincent Melluish, has a hold of Benny. His arm is gripped python like around his neck. Benny's chubby purple face shivers as he clings for his life, but it's looking like a losing battle.

"Thanks for this," says Miles calmly, "you shouldn't have, though. Really."

"Let him go Vincent," I say.

"Mr Melluish!" he roars over the sound of Benny slipping into unconsciousness.

"Mr fucking Melluish! Let him go, please."

"I'd rather not," he says, and I step into the room, "take another step, I dare you," he smiles.

Still he hasn't taken his eyes off of mine, his free arm doing everything it needs to around Benny's neck. I hold my hands up and retreat back across the threshold.

"Good lad," he says, and Benny slips away. Dead.

I turn to make some kind of plea to the CCTV, anything that will bring the dopier of the twins upstairs.

"Now, be a dear and unlock my cuff," says the resident, nodding toward the keys that dangle from Benny's belt, just out of his immediate reach. I nod, and slowly step into the room.

"Get back," I say, "I mean it."

"Told you before, if I could, then I would, but I'm really going nowhere."

I take him on his word and lower myself to the ground, my fingers picking at the key ring, doing their best to unclip them without taking my eye from the chained up resident. Once I have them in my grip he smiles.

"Would you?" he says with a smile which I return, before throwing two fingers up at him and leaving the cell, which this time I really do make sure I lock behind me, and check twice.

"Sorry Benny," I say above the bellowing from his murderer.

Gary bolts through the door to my right and into the hallway. He looks worried.

"You're lucky none of us are real," I say to him, "because Vincent just killed your pretend brother."

Gary howls in anguish, his hands to his face. Through the tears his pain turns to anger, and he pushes me hard. For the third time tonight I'm sent flying along the floor, but I suppose I deserved that, and I pick myself up without further discord.

"Gimme them fucking keys, I'm gonna tear his fucking head off!" Gary snarls, and I have no choice but to comply. He snatches them from me and slams the key into the lock hard, before almost pulling the door from the hinges.

"Ah, Gary, good to see you," says the man in the cell, "you don't look well old chap."

Gary rushes at Vincent Melluish-slash-Allen Miles, and that's all I see, because once again I slam the door closed, twisting the key in the lock, and leaving the pair of them to do what they please. I came here to do a job, and I'm fucked if I'm going to do it badly. I can explain the fucked up twins to the powers that be in the morning. Right now I've got people to see and things to do. If I'm the only one left in this building with both my sanity and the ability to breath it's my job to ensure the safety of the residents. I have a duty of care.

[119]

The clattering and yelling continues from the room, but it disappears beneath the conversation behind door seven. An American voice. Then an English one. Then Scottish. For that breath shortening, heart stopping moment I'm convinced that Wilson and Furchtenicht and fuck knows who else have broken out of their rooms and are awaiting me behind the door. Then an Irish, no, *Northern* Irish accent too. What the fuck? My hand knocks on the door before I ask it to, and the voices go quiet. Not silent. There's a whispering.

"Hello?" I call out tentatively. No answer.

"Who's in there?" My eyes flicker to the name plate. It reads *Edgerton, Les*, "Les?"

The voices mutter to one another again.

"Are you okay? Who's in there with you?" I ask as my fingers fumble around the keys.

"You aren't supposed to have anybody in your room, you know?" I say as my fingers fumble for the handle.

"Get in the corner," I instruct. I brace myself for an onrush of lunatics, my forearm held up horizontally across the front of my face. Ready to slam into the nose of the first person that attacks me. *Focus. It's your job.* The door swings open and there aren't a bunch of would be attackers.

"Les?" I ask of the lone man sitting, back straight, in a chair. His fingers tap out a steady rhythm on his knees. The man in the chair is well built, bald, and with a biker-style white moustache, which curls up as he smiles. His eyes hidden behind small circular sunglasses.

"Ain't nobody calls me Les," he says, "Jake's my name."

Fuck's sake, I don't say. Does any cunt in this building go by their own name?

"Okay? Jake, I heard voices in here with you," I say, "are you alright?"
That grin beams out again before he suddenly stops to lean forward, pulling the sunglasses down along his nose to get a better look at me.
"Shit! Foster? Who the hell let you loose? Strangers are just friends you ain't killed yet, huh?"

Life Imitates Art

By Les Edgerton

Don't play what's there, play what's not there.
Miles Davis

THE HOST tells me they currently have
twelve guests here, including me. I'm not sure if that's
a baker's dozen, which means there are really
thirteen of us or if there's just a straight twelve.

Either way, the fucker can't count for shit.
There are twelve of us in my own suite alone. That
isn't counting all the other guys I see walking around
during "free" time.

And I sure don't feel like a "guest." I feel
exactly as I did when I was a "guest" in Pendleton...
Only difference here is that I don't have a number
stitched on my shirt.

My host asked me if I'd made any friends.
"Yeah," I said. "Lots. Some really cool guys in here,
actually. Like Luke Case. Now that's a pretty sharp
guy."
"Luke Case? There's no one by that name here," he
said.
"There sure as shit is," I said. Some "host." Doesn't
even know who the other guests are. "The Limey
dude. Well," I said, considering, "*One* of the Limey
dudes. I guess that wasn't really a good description,
was it? The guy who looks like Humphrey Bogart, if
Bogart was still alive."

He got a puzzled look at that.
"Another dude I really get along with is Tubal Cain.
Now, that dude has some really scary stories. My kind

of guy. I could listen to him all night long. In fact, I do. He kept me up until four ayem last night, telling war stories."

It looked like the little light in the refrigerator of his mind started to go on.

"In your room? How could he be in your room? The doors are secured at night."

"Yeah, well you got part that right," I said. "The locked-up part. I'm just talking about the dozen of us you've got in my suite. I don't know who those other fuckers in those other rooms are, except maybe a couple I've seen in the chow hall or out in the exercise yard."

"Uh, do you know any of the others' names?"

I wasn't crazy about the way he was looking at me. Like I had a unicorn sticking out of my forehead or something. I decided to play his stupid little game, at least for awhile. The longer I could stay here, yakking, the longer before I'd have to go back to the suite. Most of the guys there I got along with and liked, except that one fucker, Alan Foster. That guy was just plain scary. The first thing he'd said to me when we met was, "Strangers are just friends you haven't killed yet." What the fuck did that mean? Whatever it meant, it didn't mean we were going to get matching tattoos, most likely. Something else struck me just then. Foster looked a lot like the guy sitting across from me. Enough to be related, brothers maybe or something. No wonder I didn't trust the fucker.

I couldn't figure him out, either. Was he in charge or what? I wasn't even clear on what I was doing here in the first place. What *any* of us were doing here. What kind of place was it anyway? In some ways, it felt like a hospital and in other ways it felt like a drug rehab place and in yet other ways it could have been a prison. Except, unless it was some kind of federal joint, it wasn't a prison. Too nice for that! Individual rooms—hell, individual *suites*. Maybe I'd lucked into one of those place where they send the Wall Street crooks? It sure wasn't a state joint. I mean, we had televisions in our rooms, a tennis court, a gym with all the crap you'd see in a high school gym, and, the biggest clue of all that this wasn't a prison—the food was outstanding. Waiters, even. Menus. Utensils, not a soup spoon you had to eat everything with. No trays, no chow line. There weren't any hacks at all. Guys in good suits all over the place, asking if you needed anything.

It was a puzzle. I didn't remember going to court for anything, having any black robe leaning over and telling me he was sending me away. It wasn't a rehab place either, I don't think. I don't remember crashing on anything—hell, all I ever did was a little recreational coke. Hadn't done anything heavy-duty in years.

No, just one morning I wake up and here I am. A mental institution, that's what it must be. The only thing that made sense. Probably had some kind of breakdown and that's why I didn't remember anything.

I decided not to sweat it. Whatever this place was and however I'd gotten here didn't much matter. The food was great, booze was everywhere, and it was like a four-star hotel. If this was the Cracker Factory, I could get used to it.

But, this guy in front of me! I couldn't figure him out at all.

He asked again, "What are the other's names? The guys you say visit you in your suite."

I ticked them off. using my fingers. "Tubal Cain, Luke Case, Alan Foster..." That name got a weird look from him. I went on. "Kori Woodson, Dave… er, Davie Diller. Davy Sheridan, Brian Morgan." How many was that? Seven. "Brian Morgan, Reg Evans…" I thought. "Oh, yeah, this guy named Tommo. I don't know his last name. Saul Stone. Two brothers— Jimmy and Sean Bennet." How many was that? A baker's dozen. There were more but I couldn't remember their names, just then.

"Those are the people you've met here?" he said. "In your room?"

'Yeah. Well, some of them. There are others." I remembered another guy who didn't talk much, just kind of sat in a corner and observed people mostly. Truman Pinter. Kind of a weird fuck. Well, not "kind of." *Really* fucked up. Which was saying something with that crew. I laughed out loud.

"What's funny?" my host said.

"Nothing," I said. "It's just…:

"Just what?"

"Nothing. Can I ask you a question?"

     He nodded.

"What kind of place is this?"

"What do you mean?"

"I mean, what kind of place is this? Is it a prison? Drug rehab? Some kind of mental hospital? What?"

"What do you think it is?"

"I asked you, man. If I had any idea of what it was, I wouldn't ask, would I?"

     He just kind of shook his head at that, like I was too dumb to live. Fuck 'im.

     He pushed some kind of button on the side of his desk and one of the suits showed up.

"George here will escort you back to your room, Les," he said. "We'll talk again."

"Les? Who the fuck is 'Les'? My name is Jake, you moron. Jake Bishop. Did you grab the wrong guy?"

[125]

That would explain a lot. But, it would leave far more questions than it answered. What the fuck was going on? Which was precisely what I was about to ask him when he held up his hand like a traffic cop and said," All in good time, Les. Or Jake. Whichever you prefer." He nodded his head to the suit and before I knew what had happened we were out in the hallway, moving toward my suite, his fingers gripping my elbow like steel tongs and propelling me along.

Don't fight it, I thought. Go along to get along. I'll figure this shit out.

Back in my suite, there were half a dozen of my new friends lounging about, drinking beer and in some cases, bottles of whiskey.

"We need to talk, guys," I said. I sat down on the sectional and they gathered around, some pulling up easy chairs and a couple sitting with me. The door opened and another guy walked in. Luke Case. He walked over and sat down beside me. "What's up, mate?" he said.

I looked at him and then the others. "Do any of you know why we're here?

Nobody spoke.

"That's what I thought. None of us have a clue, do we?"

Again, nobody said a word for a moment, and then a guy who'd just come in, Karl Black, said, "They made a mistake."

"What do you mean?" I said.

"I don't know about you guys, but the guy in charge, kept calling me Richard. Richard Godwin. I asked him who the fuck was that and all he did was smile at me. That's not my name."

Like a hive of bees, a buzz rose, everyone talking at once.

"Yeah, they did... me, too... called me Ken Bruen... who the fuck is Matt Hilton?... my name's not..."

"Okay!" I shouted. The nose subsided and they all looked at me.

"It looks like this is some kind of major fuck-up. Did anyone get called by their right name by the guy in charge?"

A unified chorus of noes was my answer.

"Me, either. I'm trying to figure out what's going on and the best I can do is that this is some kind of secret government project. Do any of you know how you got here?"

Again, a general hubbub began and the gist of it was none of knew the answer to that, either.

Little by little, we began to piece together the chain of events that had brought us all to this place. Other guys kept coming in and getting caught up. The suite soon filled up and the noise level kept rising. Finally, I shouted, "Listen up, guys!" The room quieted. It looked like I was the ipso facto leader. I took a sheet of paper from the supply furnished on the desk and wrote:

"First, let's keep it down. If this is some kind of government conspiracy, I imagine our rooms are bugged."

Everyone nodded. I passed out sheets of paper to everyone who needed it, but there were a surprising number of those gathered in the room who took out notebooks from their own pockets as well as pens. Amazing! I wondered what the odds were of a random assemblage who would have paper and pen on them.

Back and forth we went, me posing questions and getting answers.

Anyone been outside?

Two guys. Both said the same thing. It appeared we were on some kind of small island. Heavily wooded and a city could be seen across the water. Neither would venture a guess as to what city it was. The outside of the building we were in was nothing like the inside. On the outside, both men said it looked like some kind of abandoned warehouse or institutional building. Nothing like the relative opulence we were ensconced in.

Neither had spotted any boats, but we all agreed there had to be one someplace. Else how had not only we but our "hosts" gotten there.

It had evolved early on that we needed to plan an escape. It also became evident that if we were going to effect such a plan, we had the right guys in here to make it happen. It was like these guys had been planning things like this all their lives. Quickly, we'd arrived at a good guesstimate as to how many guards or "suits" there were—roughly almost two per man.

"Man!" Reg Evans whispered. "That's heavy-duty!" Amid a chorus of hisses directed at him to quiet his outburst, we all were in agreement. This was excessive. Far more than any "regular" prison. That seemed to bear out my original assessment—that this was some kind of secret government project. Who else but the government could afford this kind of manpower?

I was aware I was sweating and as I looked around could see I wasn't the only one feeling the tension.

Eventually, we settled on a plan that everybody liked. There were now twelve of in the room. There were others in the place—we had all seen them—but we agreed that they'd have to fend for themselves. When we got out, we'd do whatever we could to alert the authorities to what was going on here, but none of us were sure which of those authorities we could safely notify. Scotland Yard was the best anyone could come up with. As the only Yank there, I had to agree, although I thought Interpol might be a better bet. It really didn't matter. All I wanted to do was to beat feet and get the hell out of there and that looked to be the same mindset as the others had.

We were going to go at three in the ayem.

***

At two-thirty, I was up and dressed. I opened my door carefully and peered out into the hallway. Good. Nothing—nobody—was stirring. We'd agreed to meet up in the dining room and I made my way there in the darkness. Outside the dining room, I hesitated and then pushed the Dutch doors open and stepped in.

Instantly, all the lights came on, momentarily blinding me, and my eyes began adjusting. There at the center table, sat all eleven of my co-conspirators.

Laughing.

Hooting.

At me.

From behind me, the host himself stepped along with two of the suits. The each grabbed an arm. The host reached his arm toward me and before I could react, had plunged something sharp into my neck. I stepped off into oblivion.

The next thing I knew, I was back in his office, sitting in the same chair I had before. The only difference this time was that I had leather straps imprisoning me in the chair so that I could barely move. There was something else. All eleven of my buddies were gathered there in a circle of chairs. I was at the end. Looked like some kind of group therapy deal.

As soon as he began talking, it felt like some kind of group therapy deal.

"What's your name?" he began.

"Jake Bishop," I said.

"You see?" he said to the group of men in the chairs? They all nodded.

He turned back to me. "Your name is Les Edgerton. You're married to Mary Edgerton."

"No," I said. "I'm not. My name is Jake and my wife's name is Paris. *Used* to be Paris. She's dead."

He sighed. "I'm going to try something, Les. The truth. The truth is, your wife Mary is the one who came to us and had you committed. Do you recognize this?" He held up a piece of paper with the words:

"*Don't play what's there, play what's not there. Miles Davis.*

"No," I said.

"You should. It was taped to your monitor on your desk. It's what alerted Mary to what was happening with you."

I was getting a funny feeling in my stomach.

"Mary told us an interesting story," he said. "She told us that had become your mantra. That you repeated it, over and over, all day long.

"That you'd quit writing.

"That you'd spent all day reading. Dozens and dozens and dozens of books.

"That she was afraid you'd entered into your own fictional world. Trying to write what wasn't there. Wasn't there in real life. Trying to emulate Miles Davis."

I tried to speak, but nothing came out but a small croak. I swallowed, waited on him to go on.

"These guys?" He swept his hand, indicating the men seated around me.

"They don't exist." He waved his hand again and just like that... they all disappeared. Except one. That fucker Truman. Truman Ferris Pinter. He just sat there and grinned at me.

"Your name isn't Jake. Your name is Les. Jake is a character you invented. Paris is a character you invented. You're playing what isn't there, Les."

I almost believed him. Almost. Until Truman spoke.

"Don't listen to him, Jake," he said. "He doesn't know. He's a Philistine."

In a trice it all made sense. They'd almost caught me. Almost. Thank God for Truman. I began laughing. Truman began laughing with me. Louder and louder and more and more hysterically we laughed, and with each hoot we made, my host began vanishing, bit by bit, until finally... he disappeared entirely. What was remarkable was that with each bit of him vanishing, the others began to come back.

The chairs were filled again.

Luke Case.

Kori Woodson.

Davy Sheridan.

Brian Morgan.

Reg Evans.

Tommo.

Saul Stone.

Alan Foster.

Davie Diller.

Josh Dedman.

Rex Allen.

Truman, of course.

I couldn't control my laughter. It roared out of me, out of my throat, my nose, my very pores.

More and more people kept coming and popping up in chairs as the room filled. People I knew. Old friends.

Tubal Cain, the brothers Jimmy and Sean Bennet, Charlie Arglist, Jack Taylor, Dean Drayhart, Lupita and Dante, Elvis Cole, Black Elvis, Adel Destin, Tom Chan, Matthew Galen, Jack Taggert, Wayne Porter, Ray Midge, Roy Dillon, Metcalf the Retard, Moe Prager, Jarhead Earl, Constantine, Elliot Stilling, Tom Widmer... they just kept coming and coming and coming, filling the room and then out into the hall.

My friends...

Nine

"Who do you think I am?" I ask him for the third time, but he's clammed up.

"Uh, nobody I guess, had you pegged for some other feller, don't pay me no mind," he's saying, shaking his head.

"Who's Foster?" I ask, struggling against my own will to go in there and punch him, but there are several very good reasons why I shouldn't. First and foremost being that this looks like a man who's been around the block, and will most likely kick the living shit out of me before I've even laid a finger on him. With that in mind the rising anger subsides, being replaced by sheer frustration, "please?"

He pulls down the sunglasses from his eyes once again, and leans in. Taking the time to scrutinize my features. He frowns.

"Well, you sure do look like the fella, but on closer inspection I'd say you ain't him," he says.

"Who? Foster? Who is that?" I ask.

"Just some dude who lives here, he's a creepy bastard."

I've never heard of any Foster. Benny didn't mention him.

"I've never heard of him," I say, shaking my head. He mirrors my gesture.

"Naw, you won't have, those assholes out there call him somethin' else, same as they try to call me *Les*, but it ain't his name. His name is Alan Foster."

"What do they call him?" I ask, but I'm rewarded with another shake of the head. He mutters something. A question. Then he answers himself but with that Northern Irish lilt. He grumbles. Shakes his head violently before looking back to me, a resigned look on his face.

[133]

"Don't matter," he says, "it ain't important."

"Is it Bracha?" I ask, with no idea where that question came from. He stops his head from shaking and he stares at me. This time his eyes narrow in the darkness and he makes as if to stand up but for the first time I notice that his hands are chained to the arms of the chair. His features twist as he snarls a torrent of unintelligible abuse at me, and he pauses, panting impatiently, before he speaks again.

"See, I *knew* it was you, get the hell outta my suite! You ain't gonna kill this ol' stranger! Get out!"

Nothing makes sense. Least of all the further outpouring of abuse from the resident before me. Who does he think I am? *Why* does he think I'm that person? And who the fuck *is* that person? I cast a dejected shadow across the man tied to the chair as I quietly close his door and leave him to his fury. As the lock clicks shut he laughs. It's not just a chuckle. It's a booming Yankee laughter from a booming beast of a man. The laughter fills my brain derisively. It knows something that I don't. Fuck's sake, every fucker in this place knows something I don't. Except Benny, Benny's dead. The door vibrates against my back from Edgerton's laughter, and it send spasms into my back and neck. Makes my ear tickle. My finger guides its own way into my ear hole and rigorously scratches away that tickling itch, and as my hearing returns to normal I hear Les Edgerton cough out another laugh, and this time he speaks. It's simple, and it's cryptic.

"Blue skies, Mr Foster. Blue skies."

Who is Alan Foster?

"Hey, Jake! Would ya be quiet about your *blue* fuckin' *skies* for just a minute would ya? I can't hear myself think over here!"

Another Northern Irish accent, only, this one doesn't boom from behind the door where the man with a hundred accents resides. It's coming from somewhere else. Room eight. The last room on this floor. The hallway slides along as if was nothing and I'm standing by the door. In front of it. The slate at shoulder height reads *Brennan, Gerard.* Behind the steel there's a panting. A gasping. It's nothing like the meaty, slurping slaps of Wilson and his robotic cock. It's something else. Exercise? Is that what it is? A Counting. *Twenty six, twenty seven, twenty eight.* It's quick as a flash too. No straining. *Thirty four, thirty five, thirty six.* An upturn in tone as he passes a milestone. *FIFTY, fifty one, fifty two.* I knock.

"Come in, sixty eight, sixty nine, seventy," an almost cheerful voice beckons, I hadn't expected that, I do nothing, "I said come in fer fuck's sake! Eighty two, eighty three, eighty four."

I do as I am bidden and unlock the door. Behind it there's a wiry man doing sit ups. Not an ounce of fat on him. All tight muscle. Thick veins. Tendons everywhere. *Ninety six, ninety seven, ninety eight.*

"Don't expect me to stop here fellah, tell me what you're after and I'll tell you if I can help," he says between breaths.

"I don't know. Nothing, I guess," I say, mesmerised by the blanket of tattoos that coat his topless body. Dancing beneath the muscle that protrudes beneath the skin with every new shape the man makes.

"Then why would you bother me? Tell me that," he gasps, "it's not like I'm botherin' you now is it?"

"I just wanted to check you were okay," I say, "you know? Duty of care."

He laughs at that part.

"Duty of fuckin' care? You're a funny man so you are," he says, "one ten, one eleven, one twelve."

"Why would you say that?" I ask. Part of me thinks that Benny and Gary have been abusing these men. Not *abusing*, as such, not in the modern sense of the word. I doubt they'd get away with their cocks intact. No, I mean psychological, and physical abuse.

"Well, no offence there fellah, but you've got the biggest tits I've ever seen, you're not likely to be able to help me out, if y'know what I'm sayin'?"

I want to change the subject. I need to know about Foster, and Bracha, and all of the other shit I've been hearing. I want to ask where the fuck the staff are. I want to know what the fuck this place is, and it's as if Brennan can hear my thoughts, because he starts to speak between sit ups, and he just doesn't stop.

Lost

By Gerard Brennan

IT'S A BIT SHITE in here. I've been worse places, like. Believe me. Or don't believe me. I don't care, if I'm totally honest.

What I mean is, I don't care about your opinion. There are other things on my mind that deserve more of my energy than you do. Don't give me that look. I'm sure you're a lovely person. You're probably really good to your kids, or your other half, or your goldfish, or whatever it is that gets you out of bed in the morning. And good for you. You should be grateful. I'm grateful. Grateful that my mind is still my own. Even though on paper I might be a bit of a wee rocket, there are things we've all done that would write us off as a little... off beat.

It was just bad timing and terrible geography. Swear to fuck.

We all go through wee times of stress.

But I survived mine.

And I'm all the stronger for it.

That's how I get back at them.

I take the negative and find a way to turn it into a positive.

Like, now I have time to meditate and exercise.

The exercise is slightly limited in this space, but you know what? I couldn't do a handstand press-up before I got here. Now I can nearly do a hundred in a row. And some day I'll get to a hundred without passing out and landing on my skull.

Squats. You can do squats in a wee room like this, no bother. I can do hundreds and hundreds of those. If I had a roommate I'd ask him to jump on my back and I'd squat with a decent weight on me. I've got a bit skinny, you see. Not enough protein in our diets. I tried to supplement with things that crawl under the door. Ended up puking.

Did you notice my accent? There's some Belfast in there all right. I'm a bit of a mix. A mongrel, I suppose. Wouldn't be surprised if there was some traveller blood in my veins, truth be told. People look down on those crazy fuckers but I'd be delighted if I found out I was related. Never met a soft traveller, like. A couple of them actually helped put me in here, you know? But they were a bad example. Trust me to find the only gypsies in England that abide by the actual law of the land.

Was that a bit racist?

Didn't mean it to be.

Meant it as a compliment to their way of life.

I'm not even lying. That's one of the reasons I'm here. I never lie. It makes them uncomfortable.

Them.

I'm good at spotting the ever-present them. Rebel blood in my veins, you see. And that's not speculation or wishful thinking. There's a rich history of it in my family. Sometimes it's misplaced, but it's always there. It was simpler a generation or two ago. The oppressors hadn't learned the value of guerrilla tactics. Now they've got it down just nice. Cloak and daggers shite. None of the old waiting to see the whites of their eyes. They'll cut your throat when you're sleeping.

I don't sleep.

Working on the blinking thing.

Cameras don't blink.

You don't blink much.

There's something about you, mate. I can feel it. You're about to wake up too. Right now you're in that muzzy twilight and you're trying to remember what day it is. Here's a bit of free advice for you. Quit this job. Won't matter what day of the week it is then, mate. Gives you more time to free yourself from all the other bullshit we've been fed.

That's where I started. Jacking in gainful employment. Maybe I went at it a wee bit too fast after that. Drew too much attention to myself. *You* should try and be smarter. Then what I went through won't be wasted. History defeating, not repeating. See what I did there?

And here, don't get me wrong. I'm not telling you what to do or nothing. That'd make me worse than them. I've no right to tell you what to do, I really don't. But if you take in my wee story maybe you can learn from it. Aye, that'd be the best way to help you with your awakening, wouldn't it?

This is what I did.

The job. I don't even want to talk about that shite. Spent fourteen years at a desk and had nothing to show for it. No sense of achievement or pride. The money was almost decent, in fairness, but still. That's all I'll say about that.

The family. I'm still waiting for my missus to forgive me for jumping without a safety net. Yeah, so what I did was a bit reckless, and the kids really do need shoes, but they also need to be led by a strong role model, not some sad, soft sack of office-boy shite. She'll come around. So will the kids.

The home. I miss some of those creature comforts like an ex-smoker still breathes in the stink from the walking chimneys he passes in the street. Gadgets and toys. Distractions. I got weak.

It was a blessing in disguise when she asked me to leave.

Most men in my situation say that their wife threw them out. *Threw*, like. How fucking big are these women?

I didn't make a fuss. Just went. Packed a backpack with some essentials, tapped her for a fistful of cash from the joint overdraft, and told her she could sell the other stuff. Over the years I'd collected a lot of books. First editions, signed, rare... You'd be surprised how much you could make from a bookcase with the right kind of stuff in it. Some people are crazy, like, and would happily pay hundreds for a lump of pulp. I used to be one of them. Then I saw through it. My bookcases were anchoring me to my old life. My wife's smart enough to figure out how to make the most out of those blocks of paper and ink. She used to be an eBay ninja, before they made it near impossible to make a few quid without cutting a whole bunch of different thems in on the score.

So that was the wife and kids taken care of financially, until I could figure out how to bring the whole crew along on my adventure.

It's a work in progress, awakening, you know? A whole new game with different rules. But I'm smart. I'll learn them.

Unfortunately, as a trailblazer, it's a bit of a trial and error endeavour. Heavy on the error.

But I'm only halfway through my thirties. Plenty of time. Even taking away the stretch I spend in here out of the life expectancy equation, there'll be plenty left over. I'm sure of it.

As sure as I was that moving to England was the best thing for me. But I didn't want to just fly over to London. For a start, they'd probably mistake me for homeless in that place. And I wasn't homeless. I'd picked up a one-man pop-up tent on the way to the ferry. As a Northern Irish fellah, I figured I'd get along well with the Brits from up north. And there are all those funky accents to enjoy. I could get there via bonnie Scotland. The ferry to West Haggis-Land is more fun than a plane and the security is low. And I couldn't risk losing the big bag of weed I'd picked up after buying the tent.

I still feel a bit bad about the weed, you know. The dealer I'd found through some ever-student buddies was a pretty good guy. Friendly, smiley and chatty. Luring him away from our arranged meeting point and then pulling a knife on him wasn't very cool. He'd said so himself. But I'd spent a big chunk of my cash on that tent and I knew I'd probably have trouble sleeping until my body got used to a less pampered life.

Sure, I'll be back in Belfast some day, no doubt. I'll repay him for the insomnia medication somehow.

So, my backpack contained some clothing, the knife, a lot of weed and some other useful odds and ends. The tent came with its own wee tote bag. Barely weighed a thing. I tied it to the backpack for handiness. Totally self-sufficient, to a point.

I had to sweet talk a van-load of neo-hippies to smuggle me onto the boat. Met them at a dockside pub while I was nursing a pint and wondering how I could get on the ferry without spending the last of my cash on a ticket. They'd missed their boat and were waiting for the next one. I introduced myself and spun them a story about *the man* getting me down. Didn't get too far. Looked at me like I was talking a different language. So I offered them some free weed and promised that I wasn't interested in chatting up the girls in the group. I was only temporarily separated, after all. Showed them how I still wore my wedding ring.

They had a VW van, of course, and I was able to hide in the back under some hippy detritus. The hippies were nervous about the whole affair until I talked them into getting a bit stoned. I was cool and calm. You see, I'd taken this particular route to Scotland a few times and knew that a cursory look through the windows of a vehicle for a headcount was pretty much the height of security. Unless you were a known criminal. Then you got some hassle. Plenty of those coming and going to Old Firm matches so I knew a bunch of hippies would get an easy passage.

And they did.

It was a little rough for me, though. They didn't want me to risk leaving the van in case I got caught and we all had to walk the plank or something. The time passed pretty quickly anyway. I got extra-super high and had a root through their belongings. Found a cracker iPod stuffed with music, some of it half-decent. One of the hippies wasn't fully committed to the lifestyle as the others, it would seem. Suited me, though.

They were a wee bit annoyed when they came back to find I'd turned their vehicle into a cannabis hot-box, but we didn't get stopped on the other side, so all was well. Only their driver, the least stoned of the gang, kept going on and on about it. *We could have got caught. Enough weed to be done for dealing. It's not one bit funny. Wah, wah, wah.*

I threw the iPod at the back of his head.

It barely glanced off his dome. I'd forgotten to pull the headphones out and the lead fucked with my trajectory. Still, the point was made. And guess what.

These hippies weren't even pacifists. Fuck me, like. You can't even expect a hippy to eat shit these days. The world gets tougher and tougher.

Just a few hundred yards from the ferry terminal and I get dumped on the side of the road with what I suspected was a bruised rib and some extra lumps and bumps on my head. But they had the decency to sling my bag out after me, at least, weed and all. Good thing too. I'd have called in their number plate if they hadn't. We don't tout where I come from, but I'm pretty sure I'd have a clear enough conscious about it. I was in Scotland, like. Different country, different rules.

Scotland, yeah... Not my final destination, but a start. At least I'd crossed the Irish Sea.

Now I was headed South. Could you call that downhill? Seemed less of a big deal when I thought about it as free-wheeling or coasting or something, you know?

I walked for a while.

A good long while.

Not a lot of people are into picking up battered hitch hikers these days. I was within minutes of reeling in my thumb – although in fairness, I'd no idea about what to do after I'd quit hitching – when a seven-seater pulled into the hard shoulder. My legs were screaming for a break and my mind was numbed by weed and the monotony of tramping the same tarmac for way too long. Somehow I managed to up my pace and hobble-jog to the family wagon. I grasped the handle and heaved open the passenger door. The stench of body odour hit me like slurry fumes. I almost toppled. But I just couldn't be fucked waiting for the next highway Samaritan.

I looked around the car's interior and saw that the other six seats were empty. Shrugged and dropped my arse into the seat, slapped the dash in a friendly manner and thanked the driver for his kindness. A face that was more sweat, pockmark and frown than anything else kind of scrunched up at me. I pretended the guy wasn't as ugly as sin, forced a smile, and rubbed at my nose; snorted air through my fingers to try and filter out some of the stink. It didn't work.

The guy asked me not to slap his car. He was polite about it and all, but I was a bit narked by his fussiness. His armpits were humming like. That muskiness would be a lot harder to remove from the car than my fingerprints on the dash. But I pulled the sleeve of my jacket down over my fist and rubbed away at the spot I'd touched. That seemed to work some of the tension out of his face.

And what a face.

Now, don't get me wrong. I'm not normally a shallow person. You look a little goofy and I might actually warm to you a little quicker. I mean, pun intended, let's face it; I'm no oil painting myself. But rather that than the kind of oils that were slicking up this dude's face. Maybe I should have been choosier after all.

I asked the guy to let me out.

He told me we weren't there yet and I reminded him that I hadn't told him where I was going. Then the guy made a small error in judgement.

He grabbed a hold of my crotch.

I pushed the driver's hand away and told him politely that I was a happily married, straight man. All I was interested in was getting from A to B and it looked like we'd just about passed B. He called me a C. I laughed. Asked him if he wanted some weed.

Get this.

The dude actually called me a junkie.

Fuck me, like. A bit of weed!

Actually, don't fuck me. That was in poor taste. You know. Considering.

I gave the dude one more chance. Offered him a few quid for petrol money. Literally a few quid, mind you. Like I said, funds were low and I don't think we'd even made it a mile down the road from where he'd picked me up. He told me to shove my pennies up my hole. They were fucking pound coins, like.

So that was that.

I punched that ugly motherfucker until not even his own mother would want to fuck him anymore.

Know what I did wrong, though? Didn't wait for the shite-bag to hit the brakes. The details are a bit fuzzy from here, but the car definitely went upside-down a few times. And I'd forgotten to put on my seatbelt. I didn't go through the windscreen, though. Ended up in the backseat. Not a scratch on me, would you believe, though my balls were a wee bit tender from the manhandling. My manhandler was a mangled mess. Stuff bent the wrong way and whatnot. I saw his last breaths in the form of a blood bubble that expanded and contracted then didn't so much as pop as fall off his lips. There's a Neil Young-type metaphor in that image, but my head's not straight enough to figure it out. Maybe when they take me off the blue pills...

But anyhow. Next thing I know, the back door's been yanked open and there's this priestly looking dude staring in at me. He wasn't catholic, though. His collar was white all the way around and he wore a wedding ring. Plus he didn't grab my balls, thank fuck.

Ach, come on. Sometimes you have to go for the low hanging fruit. And no, that pun wasn't even intended.

You'd think I was a homophobe or something, wouldn't you? Just a wee joke, man.

Anyway, the vicar, or whatever he was, reached into the car and I grasped his wrist. He asked me if anything was broken before he moved me and I told him that the car and the driver were probably beyond fixing but that I was feeling pretty solid. Thank God, he said to me. I told him I'd get a run down to the chapel ASAP.

The vicar led me to his car – even carried my backpack – and I asked him if he had a phone. Saintly dude that he was, he snatched it out of his hip pocket and pushed it towards my face. An old school clamshell design. I waved it away and told him he'd be needing it himself. He looked confused until I relieved him of my backpack and reached inside. I drew out the knife, waved it in front of his face and asked him for his car keys. He told me they were still in the ignition and I bade him farewell. You know how nice that vicar was? He said he'd have no choice but to phone the cops but he'd give me fifteen minutes to get a head start.

No idea what the guy saw in me, but I'll tell you this; not all those religious types are wankers. Just like not all accountants are boring, I guess. Especially not the midlife crisis ones.

I figured if the man was going to give me fifteen minutes, I'd be sure to park up his motor safe and sound somewhere along the way. It was a nice wee thing. One of the new VW Beetles. Say what you want about pissing on the classic design, that thing was a comfortable ride. After testing the car's stability a few times with a wee handbraker or five, I did a mental calculation based on police response times back home. And I figured I'd a few hours to get as far South as I could. The vicar's Slipknot CD passed a lot of the time. I shit you not. Or slip you knot, if you prefer.

I was expecting The Proclaimers. Tried to shoehorn the five-hundred mile chorus into every Slipknot song that played. Couldn't get it to work. Those mash-ups aren't as easy as you'd think.

As I exited bonnie Scotland, I realised that the Beetle was running on diesel fumes and I was running out of patience with the driving. My head was sore and I'd puked out the driver's window at one point. The glass was streaked with swollen raisins. *When did I eat raisins?* Felt like another good boke was on the cards. So I pulled in at the next picnic area I could find. Fired up and fiddled with the sat-nav suckered to the windscreen. Found out that I'd actually managed to bypass Newcastle. By quite some distance. Looked like I was on my way to Harrogate.

So far as I knew, I'd no business in that town. I like the odd bottle of Old Peculier, like, but other than that it didn't feel like the right place at that point in my life. Besides, I was avoiding beer. Watching my figure since I'd be getting the marijuana munchies with more regularity if this adventure continued. Unless I could find a wee bottle of vodka somewhere, a toke or two would do well.

I skinned up a handful of joints; fat as fuck mind-blasters. Then I shouldered the backpack and tent, figured a snail's life probably wasn't so bad, and abandoned the car. I left the little picnic area and headed towards a line of trees. There'd be good shelter from the wind there and I could pitch my tent, start up a wee campfire and send myself on a spiritual journey from the comfort of my new home. Time to get back in touch with nature. Become one with my environment.

I lit the first joint before I found my clearing. Figured it'd hone my senses a little. Big mistake. All it did was put the heart in me sideways. Thundering pulse, jitters, paranoia.

It was around that point that I realised the pop-up tent didn't come with a pop-up sleeping bag.

Oh fuck.

I should have cried. Managed to giggle instead. And lit another doobie.

The green goodness would make everything all right. Convinced myself that paranoia was the correct state of mind for a man embarking on this kind of life-changing experience. And then the fear was gone. Just like that. I'd made it. Connected with nature. It was time to spark up the camp fire and sing hallelujah. Not literally, though. That song's been fucked in the ear so many times that it'd lost its magic. I wasn't going to flog that dead horse with another terrible rendition.

Besides, I'd probably angered God enough. Or Gaia. Or whoever the fuck rolled all this madness into a spinning marble whipping around the sun.

I put my energy into collecting twigs and leaves and anything else that looked like it'd be good for kindling. Made myself my own wee stone circle to contain the flames. Safety first, like. Then I smoked some more weed. Figured I could take a few draws then leave the remains of the joint in the middle of the twigs and leaves. Let the embers grow.

Grow.

Grow.

Crow!

Was that a crow or a raven or just a big bird that looked black because it was way too fucking dark in the woods already?

My fire didn't light. Waste of weed. Fuck sake.

I needed some of those funny-smelling fire lighters that we used to use before getting the oil in. What do you call them? Firelighters?

I decided to leave the woods. Maybe find a shop where I could splash out on firelighters or lighter fluid and try again. Packed up my unpopped tent and found a handy pocket in the backpack for the remainder of my joints. Didn't want them getting squished up and sweaty in my fist. Since it was dark my ears had gotten as sharp as fuck. I could hear traffic in the distance, figured that'd be the best way to walk. As the crow flies. Or the raven. Or whatever it was. In a straight line, anyway, instead of the zigzagging path I'd cut through the trees on the way in.

As I got closer to the sound of the traffic I started to doubt myself. Was that really the hum of engines zipping by in the night?

Nope.

It was a river.

Ah jeepers.

But I kept moving towards it. I had to see the water with my own two eyes before I could accept the fact that I was well and truly lost.

Then I started to hear voices.

Not in a schizophrenic way, though. I can hear your brain whirring right now, like. *Oh, he's been on the wacky backy for too long. It's fucked with his brain. Now he's crazy.* You do know that the link between cannabis and schizophrenia hasn't been proved, right? Google it. Government propaganda, yo.

No, this wasn't inside my head. It was outside. Like the difference between a good set of headphones and a shitty set of speakers set to mono. Especially if said speakers are in another room and there's a river running through your house.

This time I was more cautious. I held my breath while I listened. Turned on my heel three times. Slowly. On the third rotation I stopped about three quarters of the way round. The river was to my right. My mystery voices burbled down from upstream. I was certain it was more than one person. Probably as many as three. Though I couldn't make out the words, I could decipher tone and speech rhythm. Then I felt as if I was imagining it. That was the weed intruding. Had to be.

I could have called out, I suppose, but I was worried that I'd scare them away. What if they were wood nymphs or something of that nature? Supernature. Fuck that. I know leprechauns have the monopoly on pots of gold, but a nymph has to be worth something, right? Even barrel-chested male ones, as the deep cadence of their murmuring chitchat suggested.

I crept. Took each step on the tippiest of tiptoes. Made sure nothing snapped underfoot that would spook the quarry. I managed to tread so lightly I was almost tempted to test my gait on the surface of the river. But I wasn't *that* high. Stuck to the crest of the riverbank.

Then I could make out the words. Mostly chat about shitty luck. I'm not much of a fisherman so I couldn't tell you if it was salmon season or if they even had salmon in this neck of the woods. Pretty sure you'll always rustle up an aul pike in this sort of water, though. You just needed a sturdy line, a net and a damn sharp killer instinct for when the nasty bastards tried to snap at your fingers.

Closer still and I could distinguish an accent. I started to wonder if maybe I *was* high enough to walk on water. There was an Irish lilt in the chatter. Certainly there was some English in there too, but not from any region I could pinpoint. Were they...?

Fuck.

Travellers.

Irish travellers.

Poaching Irish travellers.

And as soon as I'd gotten close enough to see that there were indeed three different voices, all three owners of said voices turned to see me snigger.

At first they were as confused as me. I'd taken them for supernatural beings. Maybe they thought the same about me. Some sort of river guardian. Certainly, they didn't take me for a warden. The size and shape of these men. They'd have taken care of any lone official without a second thought.

I announced myself as a friend, but then, a foe would, wouldn't they? So the travellers didn't rush to greet me with open arms. They reeled in their lines and laid their rods on the bank. Then there was some cursing and pushing. I held my hands up as I was pinballed from one set of callused hands to the next. There was little fear in me, if I remember right. I suppose the murder I'd committed earlier had a profound effect on me. My foot upset a tub of writhing maggots and one of the men slapped my ear. That was the last straw. I popped one right in the face and skipped away from the clutches of the other two.

The traveller I'd hit laughed. So did I. The other two withdrew slightly and laughing boy wiped a line of blood from his stubbled upper lip. The quick movement created a sandpaper rasp.

His name was Big Joe. I know because one of the other two asked if he was going to go easy on me. Big Joe told his mate that there was nothing to worry about. He'd just have a little fun with me. Then he raised his fists in a boxing guard.

Oh shite.

It'd been a long time since I'd danced in the square ring. I was pretty sure this would be the end for me. The thing about a lot of these Irish travellers; they can box. They. Can. Box. Usually with bare knuckles. Some people consider it a brutal aspect of their culture. I'd always thought of it as quite a dashing and honourable characteristic. What can I say? Some people like ketchup on their fries and others like blood in their eyes.

Anyway, I raised my own hands and the two spectators cheered. We quickly established that there would be no jumping in from said spectators with a grunted exchange. I believed them, especially when the elder of the non-aggressive two offered to act as the 'fair play' man. There was a voice nagging at me – and yeah, this time it was an internal voice – trying its best to put some fear in me. No luck. I'd been in fights before where my mouth went dry, my palms got wet and my balls shrank. Typically my heart jackhammered too. Not this time. I put it down to the fact that I'd been through quite a bit that day. A wee bout like this would be child's play.

Never mind that this guy had about two weight divisions on me.

I'm an optimist.

Things got a bit murky, then.

All I really remember with any clarity is the 'fair play' man holding my head in the river water. That's not a forgettable experience. Then the pressure was off me and I could hear the 'fair play' man's screams.

Pike.

Pike.

Pike.

I crawled up the river bank. Fistfuls of grass tore away from the earth. I slipped, slid and fell flat on my face, but I made it. All the while, two men screamed.

I understood why after I coughed up half that fucking river and hauled myself up into an unsteady standing position.

The 'fair play' man had lost a few fingers.

There'd been at least one hungry pike out there looking for a midnight snack. Managed to find one. Fisherman's fingers, what? Even Captain Birdseye would have trouble marketing that one.

And then there was my sparring partner.

What the fuck happened that guy?

Looked like a pike had gotten at his face and throat, but he was bone dry.

I worked at something stuck in my teeth.

Oh. Right.

The third traveller, the youngest and smallest of the three, held a sawn-off shotgun. The business end was pointed at me.

I asked the fellah if it was loaded.

He emptied one of the two barrels. Took the legs out from under me.

Look. Scars. They're like pebbledash on my shins or something, right?

No bones broken, though. Healed right up. No idea what kind of cartridges he'd loaded that thing with, but I know I'm lucky to still have both knees. Squatting would be a bitch without them.

But yeah, I'd landed flat on my face after being shot in the shins. When I rolled over, the littlest traveller stood over me. The 'fair play' man was beside him. Both had stopped screaming. They were deciding my fate in that mad wee dialect of theirs. I couldn't keep up with the discussion so I just held tight and tried not to make too much of a fuss about their legs.

Eventually they slowed down their patter and told me that a shot to the head would be a kindness and that they had something else in mind for me.

One of them stomped on my face then. You see the kink in my nose? That's a daily reminder. Or it would be, if they'd let me have a mirror in here.

Do you have a camera phone, mate? Haven't seen myself in a while. Would be good to see how I look now. I know I must be thinner and in need of a bit of a groom. It's just that I want to make sure that the kids will recognise me if I ever see them again.

They haven't visited me yet.

But they might, right?

The last fellah that had your job said he'd try and track them down for me. Don't know what happened to him, but I think he might have been selling me a bag of shite.

Could you help me out with that, do you think?

Take some time to consider it, like. Don't feel obliged to answer right away.

I'll be here for a while yet, I'd imagine.

Yeah.

I do a lot of imagining these days.

It bugs the shit out of them because no matter what they do to me here, they can't stop me thinking. Makes a nonsense out of my captivity and they can't stand that. No matter where I am, I'm free.

I'm finally free.

Ten

"So?" he asks, still pumping his torso upright like a snake-like piston, "three fifty six, three fifty seven."

"So, what?" I say, my eyes drawn in by the square lines of shadows around each and every muscular detail of his thin, but entirely fat-free body. He snorts. "Were you even listening? I asked if you had a camera phone? I'd like to see what that shower of shite Father Time's done to my old face."

I shake my head, no, as I pat my pockets in a show of having checked, even though I know I don't. Do I? I can't remember.

"Great deal of help you are, eh?"

"Sorry," I say.

"No bother, if you don't have one then you don't have one."

"I could find a mirror?" I suggest, but hoping he declines, simply because I don't want to go and wrestle one from Richard Godwin, who won't even let me into his room. Gerard lets out a negative grunt.

Four eleven, four twelve.

"No, don't go to any trouble. Gone this long, another few hours won't make a difference."

Four forty, four forty one.

"Hours?"

Four fifty six, four fifty seven.

"Yeah, when I go for my, *therapy*. I'm sure Dr Bracha will have some sort of reflective surface I can lay my beady eyes all over."

Four seventy nine, four eighty.

"But it's," I say, bringing where my watch should be to my eye line, in order to dispute his idea that therapy will be anytime soon. Where my watch should be, but isn't. It's. It's. Dr Bracha. My mouth dries up. Gerard Brennan is far too engrossed in his exercise to notice the involuntary gasp that whistles through my nose.

Five oh one, five oh two.

The hiss of him powering through the half century easily overcomes the sound of my throat constricting and attempting to swallow what little moisture there is in my mouth.

Five twenty five, five twenty six.

"Dr Bracha?" I say as nonchalantly as I can, I cannot afford to freak the lunatic out. It's got me nowhere near an answer so far, "is he in the building?"

Five fifty, five fifty one.

"Oh aye, he never goes home that bastard," he grunts, "a wee fuckin' workhorse, so he is," he grunt, "he'll be upstairs somewhere, with the nurses."

That's the last thing he says to me as I slam the door closed. His sit-ups count never breaks pace as I lock it behind me. The corridor moves by beneath me and the CCTV camera blinks its red light at me as I approach the doors to the stairwell. Once, twice, thrice, infinity. I'm tempted to check on Allen Miles' room to see who got the better of who in the great tussle between Vincent Melluish and Gary, but not enough to stop. I have a lead. I'm a flight of stairs away from an answer. The stairs disappear behind me and I'm at the mid-level platform. Out of the window I can see that the rain has started to come down. The tip tap of the chubby droplets hammer against the window. I don't remember getting to the next floor but there I am. My hands grasp the thick steel handles of the double doors and pull. Nothing. They're locked.

Through the small glass windows I can see light. I can see movement. My hand smacks against the surface of the door. Once. Hard. Nothing, except for that tinny tubular echo which bounces from the narrow stairwell. I try again. Twice. Hard. The same echo. My fingers snake around the bunch of keys on my belt and I'm prodding each one into the lock. First one way, then upside down. Nothing. Again. One way, then upside down. Nothing. This continues for over half of the multitude of keys that fill the large ring. Then it happens. Hallelujah. Open sesame. Let me fucking in. The bolt slides from the barrel and the door opens before me. The light up here is brighter. Cleaner. It fucking well works, is the main gist of what I'm saying. Not like the ground and first floor.

I walk along the clinical, and altogether more modern looking hallway. Doors pass me by. One for a Professor somebody, doctor of something. Professor somebody else, doctor of something else. Nurses' quarters. I stop in front of that one. Brennan mentioned nurses. I knock. Nothing. My hand clamps tight around the knob, and I-

"Can I help you?" A voice calls out. A man. Another northerner. I can't see anybody though.

"Hello?"

"Who are you looking for?" the voice asks.

"Dr Bracha," I say.

"You're looking in the wrong place," says the voice.

"Where should I be looking?" I ask.

"Upstairs," the voice says. I take small and tentative steps toward the source. My shoes make sticky clacking sounds with each step.

"Who are you?" I ask.

"I go by several names," says the voice. *Of course* it fucking does. Who doesn't around here?

"And they are?"

"Well, me mam called us Gareth, Gareth Spark. But me friends know us as Langbard."

My steps continue along the hall. The nurses that Brennan promised are nowhere to be seen.

"Well, Gareth," I say, "I'm the night guard," I say, "I'm here to check on everybody, to make sure they're alright."

"Of course you are," he says, "where's that fat cunt Benny?"

"Dead. Allen Miles killed him."

Gareth emits a slight gasp. Then a hum, of sorts.

"Well, I can't say he didn't deserve it. I can't say the same for Amanda here, either."

My feet edge me further along the hall, and still there's no sign of the person that Gareth Spark's voice belongs to. Who the fuck is Amanda?

"Where are you?" I ask.

"Keep walking, you'll find us."

So I do. I edge further and further into the corridor. A door on the right is open. On the wall is the familiar slate, with the words *Spark, Gareth* upon it.

As I round the corner enough to give myself a clear view into the room the first sight I'm met with is a pair of feet. Women's feet. They belong to the headless corpse of a woman, presumably Amanda, sprawled out on the floor. A lake of blood which starts at her open neck covers the rest of the linoleum, and disappears beneath the bed upon which Spark sits. In his lap he gently cradles the head of the corpse. Thankfully the face is pointed toward his stomach, and not gasping a desperate posthumous plea to me to help her. My stomach rolls and I dry heave the nothing I had for dinner up. My knees weaken and I feel my hands slap against the hard floor as I my gag reflex continues to betray me. Spark chuckles a little, before looking down at the head.

"Well done," he says, "you found us."

The Wild Hunt

By Gareth Spark

1/

I WATCHED HER FALL by the
fence in the same way the snow fell, slowly, as though
something the world was halfway through forgetting.
I rubbed my good eye with the back of my hand, not
certain I'd seen anything at all. I hadn't been awake
long.

The forest on the far side of the valley was heavy
with snow, a still and burning silver shimmering
between my gaze and the slow turning heaven. It *was*
a girl; she raised her arm slowly, gripped the wire of
the fence and pulled herself to her knees. Her skin
was as pale as the world behind and her hair was wet
and long. A buckshot scattering of dark crimson
patterned the snow beside her. I laid the tools back in
the trailer, breathed deeply and then worked toward
her through the snow. The drift against the wall was
thigh deep and the cold ran into my boots. "Hey," I
yelled, ploughing towards her. My voice didn't get
much use and I winced at the bang of it against the
snow's silence.

She was in her late teens and barefoot,
dressed in dirt-stained jeans and a flimsy green T-
shirt thick with blood. Her hair was bottle blonde and
she lifted her face towards my voice as though
sensing the heat of it, a creature turning to face the
current it has to fight. Her left eye was swollen purple
and scarlet and blood had dried beneath her nose and
across the delicacy of her jaw. Pale channels marked
the progress of tears through the grime across her

face. She gripped her side with a wet, red fist and whispered something in a tongue I didn't know. Her voice was dry and small. I stood above her, glanced around at the forest and the low-lying land beside the river; nothing moved beside the steady snow.

I pulled the jacket from my shoulders and draped it around her. There was a stink of sweat and blood above the electric sharpness of winter falling upon itself. She jerked away when I touched her and I lifted my hands, palms facing her, hoping to show I was no threat. "That's all right," I said, "I'm OK, you see? It's all right, but you have to come with me, love, out of this bloody cold, you really have to."

Her skin had a crystal blue tint, the first sapphire flush of hypothermia. 'You've got to let me help you,' I said, moving towards her, as you'd approach a dog you can't trust not to snap. Cold sank through my shirt, a wet chill, as though I'd collapsed through the surface of a frozen pond and the first thrill of ice had faded, leaving only the heavy draw of winter.

She gripped my shoulder, lifted herself up and snarled with pain. The snow sat about her hair and melted in her blood-filled lashes and she looked at me, and then glanced away. I accepted her weight. "That's it," I said, gasping the words a little, as my wet boots sought purchase beneath the powdery snow. There was no wind, no light on the land save the sour sun sieved through cloud thick and dark as tarnished steel. 'That's it, come on.'

She inhaled sharply through her mouth at the first step, and then whispered through the wet frame of hair fallen across her face. The girl stumbled through the snow and I felt her tremble against the joint of my shoulder.

It brought to mind a young doe I ran down, during the spring. I remember I killed the engine, climbed into the green night, knelt in the starlight glow of the back road and laid a hand on the creatures flank as it died. I felt the thud of the doe's final heartbeat and a tear burned from my good eye for the first time in twenty years. There were even tears in the socket where my left eye had once taken the world. It surprised me you could weep from nothing, over nothing.

The snow was heavier now, relentless as only things offered by the sky can be relentless; flakes that were brilliant as candle flames flickered against the sky. I glanced at the girl's naked feet; they were raw, painful, and shone as if stones polished by the rain. She mumbled in her strange language; it was a feathery, melancholy incantation. "Where you from, love?" I asked. I needed to keep her alert.
She said, in English, "I can't believe it."
 "What can't you believe?"
 She didn't reply.

The truck and trailer stood by the fence I set out that morning to repair. It was a broad, fallow field, the last of my land before the National Park. The vehicle slanted on a rough track, dark beneath its frosting of snow. I reached for the door with my free hand. The girl's weight pulled at me and in spite of the cold, I felt the prickle of sweat beneath the band of my old baseball cap. My gloves were slick and I missed the handle once before managing to click it open. "In you get," I said, pushing the girl with my shoulder. Her legs draped out of the side and I saw she was near enough unconscious. I lifted her feet into the vehicle. There was an old wool blanket inside the footrest and I spread this across the girl. She sat up and glared at me. Her unwounded eye shone bright green flecked with gold and I knew she wasn't looking at me but at something far off, something only the dying recognised.

I smiled at her nonetheless and asked, "What's your name? What do they call you"' She lay back without answer. "Fair enough," I said and pushed the door closed. I headed to the rear of the truck and uncoupled the trailer.

"You have trouble now," I said, glancing down at the valley and the slow steel of the river. "Lord help us, you've got nothing but trouble."

I drove steadily down the track and onto the dirt road for the hills. I got out, closed the gate behind me. Gristhorpe stood on the opposite side of the valley; a glow of lights turned against the January dark. Behind was my place and miles of snow-struck forest. I climbed back in, turned the vehicle left on the road, steering for the channels cut by passing tractors through the snow, twin black lines leading through the blizzard. The steady stream of blood leaking from the girl's side electrified the frigid air and I felt an old sick feeling, one that hadn't troubled me for more years than I cared to put together. A ghost rose behind my concentration, a face that usually lay quiet in a grave of years and forgetfulness and I shook my head as a dog might shake away the rain.

The pines growing either side of the gate leading into my place were lost in the blizzard. I left the engine running and climbed out into the grey world. The old iron of the massive gate burned my hand as I heaved against its dead weight, swinging it back into the trees with a mournful creak. The brim of my hat was thick with snow and I took it off and shook it hard as I walked back to the vehicle. The headlights beamed through the curtain of snow and I got in, looked the girl over and drove a hundred yards to the old farmhouse. The skeleton of a barn, roofless and naked to winter, towered behind the low slate roof of the house. A six-foot high tower of tractor tyres, an old Nissan on bricks, the ruin of a washhouse, a trailer grimed white and grey, a square of hay beneath a tarpaulin for the horse; my place wasn't that great. The house was on the eastern side of the yard, Skelder Moor behind it, stark against the sky; the stables and the sour fruit smell of dung, hay and horse breath. Pools of ice thick before the stable doors, hoof prints glittering in the pale morning.

I headed to the porch, unlatched the door and went back for the girl.

She slid on the cigarette burned leather with a moan. "Come on," I said. Blood ran in rivulets across the beige hide of the seats. She whispered as I lifted her from the vehicle and I felt the snap of pain in my gut, thought I was going to drop her, then settled myself square on the slush, mud and churned up horseshit of the yard. Took a step, grunted, swallowed back a pang of regret for the lost strength of my arm and trudged heavily to the door. I was getting old after all, lucky to have reached the age I have, tired most mornings and every single night, alone upon the earth.

I kicked the door open; the dog came out like a black-furred cannonball. It licked at my wet jeans and barked in relief at my return. I stumbled against the stupid thing. "Go on," I said, "get on." The dog, a greyhound mixed with something questionable, shot a look with eyes of wet ebony and dashed past me into the snow.

The parlour fire burned low; powdery grey ash flecked here and there with embers now glowing hot in the draught. The dog's basket lay in the corner, a mess of blankets and chewed rubber toys. I felt the tendons in my elbow pull as I lay the girl on the sheepskin rug before the fire. "OK," I said, 'just you lay there, love I won't be a minute.' The fire popped and a cinder hit the fireguard. I watched the girl's breathing. Her yellow hair spread over the moth-eaten rug as if that of somebody pulled from the sea. Her breath came in little silver clouds in the parlour's gloom.

I filled an electric kettle in the kitchen, flicked the switch and steadied myself against the worktop. The dog yapped outside, scratched at the door and the clatter of claws brought me out of the fatigue filling me from a broken place inside, a place I ignored most other times.

Two rubber hot water bottles hung from a hook on the back of the bathroom door. I grabbed them, dashed back for the kitchen as the bubbling growl of the kettle grew. The dog howled outside in the snow. I held the tip of the first bottle between the tines of a dining fork over the sink and carefully tipped boiling water inside. The hot rubber smell of the bottle filled the room as I squeezed the air pocket out of it before screwing in the plastic stopper, tight. I did the same with the next, then darted into the parlour and lay them between the girl's arms and her body. You have to warm the core first, with hypothermia. If I set the warmth directly onto the girl's stark blue feet, it most likely would have sent her into shock. Taking her wet clothes off would have been the right thing to do as well, but I had no dry clothes to offer and, it felt wrong; I couldn't do it. She moaned. I shuffled on my knees, lifted away the mesh guard and tipped a little coal from the brass scuttle onto the glowing mess. It hissed and darkened and dust seeped between the cold lumps as flames built from below.

The girl groaned again. Her eyes flickered. I hobbled into the kitchen and, using the morning's filter, set a new pot of coffee to go. Then I went back into the parlour, paused and glanced over at my reflection in a broad, heat-stained mirror above the fire, as though the mirrored double would know what to do in a purer way. One eye was a cicatrice of ruined flesh and the other twinkled back, blue and wide. "So," I said, "you're going to have to look." I knelt and, perhaps with too much caution, lifted the green shirt from the girl's wounded side. "Yeah," I said, resigned. A long and very deep cut gaped open in her pink flesh, the meat red and butcher fresh inside, the wound perhaps ten inches long and an inch deep, as though inflicted by a Stanley knife, something wickedly sharp, but not long enough to damage anything vital. Hypothermia and blood loss, a lethal combination; I lay a hand against the girl's face. The wickedness of the world always surprised me, and I never understood why. She opened her eyes, vivid and green as spring grass.

"You all right, love?" I asked

She muttered something in her language. Then, as though remembering, she started again in English, "They are coming."

"What was that?"

"They are coming."

I looked over at the white sky beyond the window outside. It was snowing again, and the wind was picking up. A storm was on the way.

2/

I bandaged her up well as I could with the old bits and pieces left over in my first-aid kit and waited as life came back to her. Tried ringing the police but my mobile network was down and it's been years since I had a landline. I thought about leaving her and heading over to the village or the closest farm at the foot of the moor, old Gallon's place, but the reality was I was isolated. There was nothing up here on Skelder Moor but silence, and me. Therefore, I decided to wait, see if the storm passed and, if it did, drive her down to Gristhorpe.

She rose about the same time the light fell, slowly, painfully, her shirt crisp with dry blood. She touched her side, winced and stared up at me for what felt a long time. Then she asked for water.

I fetched a splash of tap water in a tin cup and offered it to her. She drank slowly and then cast an eye at the darkness welling against the window.

"What is the time?" The accent fell across her words as though light, colouring the blocky Anglo-Saxon phonemes with something almost ethereal.

"That doesn't matter, we have to ring the police."

"Who are you?"

"Langbard," I said, "who did this to you?"

She glanced over at the fire and there seemed a subtle shift in the light of her eyes, as though they were glass, with nothing behind. "It matters only they are coming, they are hunting."

"Why? Who the hell's hunting you?"

"Bad things," she said.

"Then we need to get to the police."

"The police?" She laughed, and then winced as the pain struck again. I wondered if she was still a little delirious. There was no colour to her flesh. "I think not, man."

That made me smile. "Have you taken something? Been out partying somewhere and wandered away?" It seemed the most likely solution; New Age travellers sometimes gathered at stone circles on Skelder Moor to get off their heads on mushrooms or acid or whatever kids did these days to make the world go away, but not with the temperature well below zero and the worst storm of winter on its way. I listened to the wind howl, and wondered if there were more bodies up there, in the dark.

"What happen you eye?"

"My eye?" I lifted a hand and touched the scarred flesh self-consciously. "An accident, when I was a boy."

"Really, what really happened?"

The question was a strange one I attributed to her second-hand knowledge of the language. "I told you," I said, "an accident." I thought back to a day that was burned in me, and, for the first time, couldn't picture it, the bike, the twisted metal, the smash on the high road. It was as though I was looking at something through a haze of smoke, the lines were fading, broken up, and for a terrible moment, it was as though the whole world shifted. I saw that face again, remembered the name behind it, the wedding day three months before and the way she said my name. I killed the thought, pushed it down below things I could hold onto, the stink of burned steel, petrol, a summer's day and the pain, I could take those, but not the name, nor the memory. Not those blue eyes and Judy, Judy gone forever, "It was a motorbike," I said, more to myself.

"They're coming," she said, "we should go."

"Who are 'they'?"

"I told you, bad things."

I nodded. The years have taught me patience, if nothing else. I reached for the packet of Lambert and Butler on the sideboard, lit one and breathed the smoke deeply. The wind howled in the trees outside and the girl glanced at the glass. "You're afraid," I said.

"Yes."

"What's your name?"

"My name is Huldra," she said quickly. She had been sitting on the floor before the fireplace and now, with much effort, she pulled herself up to her feet, "and you must listen to me. We have to get away from the moor."

"Now listen, love," I said, "I've lived me whole life here and there's nowt on that moor but old stones, heather and bloody sheep. If you've fallen out with your boyfriend or whatever, I don't mind putting a roof over your head for the night. I don't know what drugs you took, or how much you drank but...." The dog distracted me. Its hackles rose suddenly and it stood in the corner, cowering. I drew on the cigarette. "Summat's spooked the auld lad."

"They're coming."

"Stop saying that."

"The host, they're coming," she whispered. Then she smiled. "Perhaps I should leave."

"You're in no state to walk anywhere, love, and it's cold out there enough to knock you stone dead, you in your bare feet too. The closest place is Gallon's, eight miles down the road, and we aren't going there."

"Why can we not?"

"It's a long and old story, one you don't need to know."

"Then you will die too."

I stared at her for a long time. The fire popped and sparked beneath the dog's whimpers. I rushed the cigarette out into an old pub ashtray balanced on the arm of the chair.

Then everything went black.

Power cut; the room plunged into a darkness relieved only by the dwindling fire. I heard the fridge in the far room fall silent. Then there was nothing but the wind, an ocean of air crashing the snow in waves against the stone; trees bending back so far you almost heard them scream. A power cut now was the last thing I wanted.

"Bollocks," I said, standing, slowly.

I heard the girl breathing in the dark and saw, briefly, her eyes flash like a cats. She was saying something in her language, something that sounded like a prayer. There were candles in the dresser and, as I searched for them, I yelled at her over my shoulder, "Will you stop that bloody chanting, I'm trying to think here." She fell silent. The dog whimpered. I lit a candle with the bic lighter and, as the flame sparked into life, it revealed Huldra, inches from me. Her overlarge green eyes and almost white hair caught in the sudden glow seemed uncanny, and the hair stood to attention all along the ropy tendons of my neck. "Listen," she whispered

I was confident then that whatever happened to her on the moor, whatever Hells-Angel- brewed acid she dropped had cracked her wits. "Listen to what?"

There was no noise outside the storm, nothing but the barrage of hail against glass, gust against stone and then, as though something far away that was approaching quickly, I heard a sound like the end of the world.

It put me in mind of an old-fashioned horn they used on foxhunts back when, only with a power, a strength that tore at you. It pierced the weather and the night and the world, a growing scream of something in the tempest, something rising with a crash of darkness.

I only realised I'd bit through my lip when I tasted blood. "What the fuck is that."

Huldra glanced at me, then turned and dashed for the door with a speed I thought her injury would deny. The dog snapped at her ankles as she passed. "Wait!" I yelled, but was too late.

She had fled into the night.

3/

        I pulled an old sheepskin jacket round my shoulders and looked out through the kitchen door into the yard. The great black mass of the moor appeared and disappeared behind the surging grey wall of snow and the forest on the far side of the white road twisted and roared as if something trapped. I squinted into the cold breeze, and yelled the girl's name. The prints of her bare feet led away through the crisp white snow towards the trees, and beyond that, all was dark. I'd known bad winter storms before, many, too many of them to recall, but there was something different about this. It seemed purposed, as though some malign intelligence lay behind the way it swept down from the snow-wrapped moor. Then there was the girl, off her head, certainly, but barefoot and half naked and out in the teeth of winter on a night you can't see more than five foot in front of you; she seemed so convinced something was following, that 'they' were coming, I admit, it had rattled my cage more than a little. I walked back into the parlour and my hand lingered before the double barrel shotgun bracketed to the wall. I had sworn never to use it except in the direst of circumstances, but the girl's panic had an earnest quality that suggested taking the gun might just be the proper thing to do. Her pursuers could turn out to be meth-fired bikers, crazed cultists, any bloody thing. There was a dust-streaked box of shells on top of the kitchen cupboard and I slipped two into the chambers, pulled on my flat cloth cap and stepped out after her.

The storm howled about my ears. I heard loose tiles chatter like teeth on the roof of the farmhouse and the eerie screech of the forest and nothing else. Usually you could see the distant lights of the village but now there was just darkness, a deep oleaginous gloom slipped behind the whirling snow like a skull behind skin. I shouted her name a couple of times, the dog at my heels, tail jammed between his legs; his coal dark fur had filled with snow, he glanced up at me, the whites around his eyes showing clearly, and I heard that noise again, the horn. It sang down from the moor, out of the air itself, it seemed all around me, the boom of falling ice, the long drawn out note was electrifying, and I held the gun in front of me and looked up and around, but could see nothing.

Then I caught sight of him, standing in the lee of the barn, shivering, a scarf wrapped around his long sallow face, old Gallon, from the next farm down. He was crouched against the wet timbers, his teeth chattering. He saw me and waved and I trudged through the deep snow towards him. "You," I said, "what you doing up here?"

"Power's out," he yelled above the storm.

"You got here fast."

"No, I were driving past, heading home and me 4x4 cut out dead as you like, right outside of here. Same time I saw your lights go down. She won't start, nothing, no lights, no nothing. I was going to walk on, you know I don't want to be here, but I saw summat ... up there." He pointed to the moor behind.

"What did you see?"

"I don't know what it was," he said. Then he looked into my face for a moment, his grey beard filling with snow. "Ever think of her?"

"Pete, don't be a silly beggar."

"A silly beggar, am I? You killed that girl."

"It was an accident."

"She was my sister, my only family."

The horn sounded again and Pete Gallon, a farmer of 40 something years' experience, clapped his gloved hands either side of his head. I shook his shoulder and said, "I need your help, there's this lass wandering round out here. She doesn't have a clue what she's doing, I don't think she's a full shilling, but she'll die if we don't find her. Help me look for her." He nodded, staring down at his feet, seemed to collect himself. "Why have you got the gun?"

"Long story."

"I don't like this, none of it. You reckon you're chasing some lass out here, you've a gun, my ride breaking down and that I saw, up there."

"What was it?"

He frowned, seemed to search his memory. "I can't say."

"You can't?"

"I mean there are no words to fit it into."

I pointed to the footprints that were filling with snow. They led into the ancient forest stretching from the moor to the coast. Officially named the Mansfield Estate, we always knew the woods as Fosse Grim.

4/

It was hard going for two gents on the wrong side of 50, as Pete and I both were, made even harder by the fact we hadn't spoken for a couple of decades. His tracking was always superior to mine when we were younger, snaring pheasants and rabbits in Fosse

[173]

Grim, and he followed the girl's progress through the thickly gathered trees where there was no sign, or indeed trail, obvious to me. He would point out a snapped twig, a dislodged stone, the print of a heel in beck-side mud and grunt. I followed meekly as the tempest roared through the skeletal boughs above, blasted white on the windward side by snow, black and wet on the other. Once or twice, I thought I heard something above that relentless cacophony, a thunderous growl that came up through the soles of my feet as though we were at York races and the horses were charging by us. Then, I thought I'd seen a light behind, in the immense twisted darkness of the forest, a green light that I caught at the very edge of my vision, only briefly, but enough to impart the sensation that it was a flame, a rolling green flame boiling between the dark trunks of winter dead oaks and sycamores. "Pete," I said.

He hushed me. "We're near Pen Howe."

Pen Howe was a tumulus in the heart of the wood, a Bronze Age monument forbidden to us as children because of the singular evil with which it was associated in folklore.

"She reckoned she was being chased," I said. The teeth chattered hard in my skull and the iron of the gun burned through the wet wool of my gloves.

Pete turned to face me. "By who?"

"I told you, she's not right in the head."

"How she's kept going through this snow on bare hooves is a mystery to me," he said.

"Drugs can make people perform rare physical feats."

"'course I never had your schooling. Some of us worked farms while others pissed off to University."

"The girl could be dying, Pete."

He sighed so loudly I heard it above the crack of dry branches in the gale. The snow flew almost sideways through the primeval wood., and I squinted into it as though a handful of grit had been thrown into my face. "You stay here," he said. "It's a dead end with the cliff behind the Howe, if she comes back this way, stop here."

"Do you want the gun?"

"No," he said, "I'd be too tempted to use the bugger on you when I got back."

I laughed at his scorn. He stroked his wet beard, pulled the hat lower onto his brown and pushed his way forward through trees that were grey with spattered snow. The air stank as though something was burning but there was another odour beneath it, like that of a badger trapped in a set, savage, rank and dangerous. I supposed something was dead out there among the trees. "You smell that?" Pete shouted back.

"I do."

"Keep your eyes open and have a care not to shoot me coming back." He stepped a few more paces through the drifting snow and called back. "What do they call this girl, by the way?"

"Huldra."

He laughed. "That's not a person's name, mate." Then he stepped below the bank and I lost sight of him.

I crouched beside ivy wrapped oaks and gazed into the gloom. The breaths escaped me in long silver clouds and I watched them dissipate into the wind when I heard the roar above me and felt a gust that knocked me flat into the icy mud and then I saw them.

At first, I thought it was a flock of geese lost in the storm, grey bodies writhing above the trees against the larger black of night. Then I realised no bird moved as these things were, no birds twisted and struggled and twined around each other the way these grey things did. The forms darted as though mercury through cloud and the ghost of the storm, and I heard the sound again, that horn. This time the earth shook beneath its screech and I felt something pop in my ears and, Lord help me, if I didn't scream. Then they had passed, and I had the sensation something of great power and size had passed, as though I was a small dinghy in an ocean bobbing in a battleship's wake. I struggled to my feet, using the gun to push myself up and headed over the bank towards the Howe. A green glow ahead flickered through the trees, shimmering in the ice frozen across puddles on the track where Pete had stumbled.

Then I heard him scream and a shape blundered ahead of me. I fired from the hip and the figure fell back down the bank just as I cleared it. I saw Huldra at first, and then I saw the huntsman. She lay across his shoulder. Her arms flailed towards me and she screamed for help. I had the impression of a hundred things moving behind them in the trees, grey shapes with red ears and eyes like frozen lightning, then I lifted my gaze to the huntsman himself, high above the ancient Howe. His outline shifted like smoke and the green fire flickered around his feet. He wore grey furs and long grizzled hair hung around his shoulders. At his side, a vast, bloodstained horn hung from a wet leather strap and two ravens clacked and screeched as they circled just above him. Huldra screamed and screamed and then the huntsman, as though noticing me at last, glared down and I saw, with a rising horror that sucked at my heart and drew every dreg of warmth from my bones, that it was my own face staring back at me.

I jammed my eyes shut and felt a hot wind filled with dust rip through the winter and I heard Huldra cry a final time. It was a shattering scream; as if the whole world had distilled its collective despair into a single note.

Then there was silence.

I crawled across to Pete. He lay on his back on the bank side and the snow beneath him was turning a crimson that was almost black. Both barrels directly in the face had taken most of his skull away. The air stank of blood and flame and the wind died suddenly. I looked over to the place I had seen the huntsman and saw nothing.

I was alone in the woods with the man I'd killed, and that's how they found me the next day.

Eleven

Another dry heave attempts to get vomit from my stomach that simply will not come. I make an effort to pull myself upright but it's useless. The scene in front of me has knocked me for six. Spark chuckles again, looks down to the head in his lap, hushes it quietly as he strokes the woman's hair.

"There are a few more like her around here. You know? Dead like? Don't blame me though, it was the alien," he says, shaking his head.

"Alien?" I gasp, trying to look him directly in the eyes but the carnage in my peripheral vision drags my line of sight directly back to the headless corpse, "Oh God," I mutter.

"Yeah, he's a nutcase like," he says, "a proper nutcase. Everything was great until *he* showed up."

Rather than try to stand I shuffle around and pull myself onto my arse, with my back to the doorframe. My head drops slowly until it hits my knees. *Alien?*

"Is the alien why you're here?" I ask. Spark shakes his head.

"Were you not just listening to ma story? I told you why I was here already," he sniffs, "am not a lunatic like, not like the alien."

"Who's the alien?"

"You couldn't pronounce his real name."

"Where is he?"

"Probably back in his room. He went off on one when, uh, Benny unlocked the doors, probably tired himself out."

"*Benny* let you out?"

"Uh, aye," he says.

"Why?"

"Dunno," he says, his eyes searching for the words, "he just comes up, says we've to scare the new fella, which I'm guessing is you. Unfortunately he let the alien go too, and he got a bit of stuff off his chest like. You know? Killed Amanda and the other nurses. Shame about- I mean, uh, where is Benny?"

"Dead."

"That's a shame."

"Yeah," I say. So Benny let them out to frighten me. To scare me off of the job. Send me packing. I suppose that makes sense. Kind of.

"Did *you* kill him?" he asks. I shake my head, no.

"Allen Miles did," I say, drawing a knowing nod from Spark.

"Not surprised, Vincent's a mean fucker. Him and Benny never really got on."

The conversation has calmed my nerves just slightly, and I'm moved to attempt to stand. I continue to keep my eyes on Gareth Spark's, and with one hand I steady myself against the door frame.

"Do you know about Gary?" I ask, in between sucking in deep breaths. Spark nods.

"Aye, number two of the Twin Towers," he says, "I've mentioned him to Dr Bracha before but you always get that same look, that one that says he thinks you're talking shite."

"Where is Bracha now?" I ask.

"I told you, he'll be around upstairs," he shrugs, "he's only ever upstairs. He might come down if you ask nice like."

I move away from door, and my hand reaches for it. Spark shuffles slightly in response to this, and makes to move from the bed. At this point my gag reflex is tested once again as he pulls his erect cock from the mouth of Amanda's skull. The head drops to the floor with a dull thud and Spark grapples with his cock, desperately trying to trouser the thing. Before he can stand properly I've slammed the door closed. I try to

[179]

hold the thing closed as I finger the keys frantically looking for his. He's at the other side screaming blue murder at me, trying to pull the door open. The key presents itself at the perfect time as he steps away to regain his energy, and me locking the door is given a soundtrack of swearing and threats. I'm hoping to God that he quietens soon, because I need to find, and lock whoever *the alien* is away, before something else happens.

I round a corner, and see exactly what Spark was talking about. There are the bodies of the nurses strewn everywhere. Some naked, others with clothes torn at unfortunate places. I get a shortness of breath and try to focus. This can't be happening. I want to check them for vital signs, or cover their poor modesty in death, but I've seen enough police-based shows, and read enough books to know that you don't mess with a crime scene. One hair of mine in the mix is enough to incriminate me forever, and then what? I'll be in here, as a resident. That's what. The floor is caked in sticky, rapidly drying blood. Small dry islands of bare footprints help me to navigate to where the actor of such violence is housed. As I step as carefully through the blood as possible there's a soft breathing sound coming from the open room. It doesn't come from an alien, far from it, but the person that sleeps there is undoubtedly a monster. He's covered from top to toe in the blood of his victims. I pull my keys out carefully and quietly, as I look for evidence of who this person is. The door says *Stanley, Martin*, so I search out the key with MS written across it in the same familiar fine point permanent marker pen. The monster stirs. His tongue slaps hard against his teeth and his bloody hand scratches at some sleep-itch on his chest. I need to secure this one. I really need to secure him. Then I need to call the police and get this whole situation finished with. I can't handle it. My first day and I've met some of the most fucked up beings that ever walked the Earth, I've been screwed over by my new colleague and his secret twin, and to top it all off I've got a murder scene on my hands. This was not in the application. I can't even remember filling out the application, but I can pretty much guarantee that none of the above was part of the job description.

With the key already primed in one hand, I step over the threshold to try to quietly pull the door closed. Martin Stanley stirs, so I throw caution to the wind and get a little bit hastier about proceedings. The latch drops into the barrel and I lock the door as calmly as I can.

"What are you doing?" says a voice from behind the door. Stanley? That would be impossible. The man was fast asleep, "you can't just go around locking people away. I have rights."

I don't say anything. The voice speaks again.

"You've got the wrong person. I'm not here to hurt anybody. I'm here to help you. All of you."

I say nothing.

"I shouldn't be here," says the voice.

I say nothing. Then the man behind the door emits a strangled wails, like nothing I've ever heard before. Not even from Keith.

"I really shouldn't be here!"

Once again, I say nothing.

The Matryoshka Doll

By Martin Stanley

I shouldn't be here.

Now, I know what you're thinking: Don't they all say that?

Maybe, but that's not the point.

I'm not crazy, like the others. I hear their moans in the night, echoing down the corridors, bouncing inarticulately off the surfaces. Occasionally, I feel the thump of my neighbour in my bones as he throws himself against the wall. Every time he does it, I tell myself that I don't belong here.

Hell, listen to them all, screaming about the lights. Idiots. Now listen to me, quiet, rational and calm – do I sound like a loon?

I'm clearer in mind and spirit than you are, friend. I know who I am and who I'm not.

Can you say the same?

They've made a mistake. I don't belong here. I'm not even human.

Now, I don't mean that in the metaphorical sense, but in its full literal meaning. I'm not human. I'm an alien life form.

Don't give me that quiet, patronising sigh – thank you very much. I know what I am and where I'm from.

Of course, I could give you the name of my planet, but then I'd have to kill you – I'm on a top-secret mission, after all. We've been watching you for a long time, you human beings, ensuring that you don't have the means to leave this little ball of water and rock that you call home.

Did you know that you're the only species in the universe that's incapable of co-existing peacefully with others? On every other planet we've visited, the life forms occupy their habitats in harmony with each other – if the balance starts to tip some natural correction occurs and order is restored. Humans are the exception: far too selfish and short-sighted to even understand what balance means. Humanity's nothing more than a virus with a brain and opposable thumbs.

If you had the technology to occupy other worlds you'd be the most dangerous creatures in the universe. Your savagery is boundless, and it's only your inability to think ahead that's your saving grace – you'll probably destroy yourselves before *we* have to.

We've been sent here to monitor the news, the people, the scientific and technological communities for evidence of progression, for signs that mankind might be a species worth saving, for any sudden technological advances that might affect us.

Oh, you're wondering how we get here, right? Well, it's to do with wormholes, see? Or at least, that's how you perceive them. The universe is made up of these things, only you can't see them. They come and go so quickly that the human eye can't register them, although the brain does process them as déjà vu. We can skip worlds in seconds and traverse entire galaxies in the time it takes you to commute to work in the mornings. The only thing is, we can't make the leap in vehicles, or in our own flesh; the sheer force of a wormhole would fold a metal object a mile in length to the size of a bullet and flesh would be destroyed completely. So we have to send our consciences, our essence, if you will, our souls, to your planet via these wormholes. And once we're

[183]

here we need to quickly take possession of a host – we have a five-minute window – before our chance is gone and we're catapulted back into our bodies.

When I took possession of Martin Stanley, he was running. I didn't know why – not at that point, anyway. Sweat rolled down his red face, which was frozen in a rictus of fear, and his head twitched from left to right, as though looking for something. His gut bounced beneath the blood and sweat drenched T-shirt he was wearing. His baggy jeans were caked with mud and gore. He weaved without coordination through the trees, stumbling over loose branches and wiry knots of wild grass. Every time he took a bad step he let out an almost girlish squeal of fear.

I made the leap into him, taking possession of his mind.

It was then I realised why he was running. It was then I realised my mistake. This man was a monster, the kind of creature that populates nightmares.

I slowed down to take in my surroundings. I felt the arrhythmic beat of his unhealthy heart, the harsh rattle of his lungs, the burning of muscles overloaded with lactic acid. Most of all, I was overwhelmed by the darkness that consumed him, the horrors that lurked in his head. I wanted to leave his body, but once contact has been made it can't be unmade. Only death can break the bond.

A cacophony of voices came from me.

"There's nowhere for you to run."

"Stop."

"We can help you."

"Think of the families."

"Come here, you piece of shit."

I didn't yet realise what he'd done, only that there was something awful within him. I tried to move faster, but his muscles had nothing left, and he collapsed on the floor. Before I had a chance to look at his pursuers they were upon me, inflicting punches and kicks, striking me with objects, their blows vicious and without mercy. I remember screaming in pain. And as I slid into unconsciousness, I hoped that one of these blows would kill me, so I could return to my home world.

I woke several hours later, both hands cuffed to a hospital bed. A young nurse looked at my chart and shook her head. She was unhappy, mostly because I was going to live and make a full recovery. I remember the images that ran through my head, which still had traces of the host locked away in its darkest recesses. I felt a desperate urge to hold her down and slap away that look of contempt. This was followed by the desire to slice her clothes off with a surgical scalpel and take her until she screamed in pain, until...

Bile rose up into my throat and stayed there until I swallowed. The bitter, metallic taste lingered, reminding me of the thoughts I'd had. I needed to wash the taste and the thoughts away.

When I asked her for a drink, she spat in my face and stormed out. Though I wasn't alone for very long.

A tall police officer entered the room and stared at me with a sneer of contempt. He moved beside the bed and prodded one of my bruises. The pain made me want to cry out, but instead I just whimpered.

He leaned forward until his mouth was inches from my ear.

"You better start talking, son," he whispered. "Tell the families what they wanna know."

"But I don't know anything," I said. And I didn't, not at that point, anyway. The process of absorbing my host's mind wasn't fully complete; so there were huge

[185]

gaps in memory and logic, with entire branches of his life still a mystery to me.

The officer didn't believe that. Gritting his teeth, he wrapped his hand around a bruise on my forearm and squeezed with all his might, until I passed out. Then he slapped me awake, though not hard enough to leave a mark, and said: "There'll be a lot more of that if you don't start telling us where they're buried, you fat sack of shit."

When they moved me to a cell a few days later, I knew pretty much everything there was to know about Martin Stanley. And the more I discovered, the more trouble I realised I was in.

A fat detective with mottled skin and three-day stubble sat beside his thinner, paler partner and stared at me. A young, scruffy legal aid solicitor sat to my right and occasionally whispered orders in my ear: answer the question, don't answer it, let me talk, the usual.

The fat detective leaned across the table slightly whenever he opened his mouth. "We've found the three you buried out in Whitewebbs Wood," he said. His jaw muscles danced and popped as his mouth pursed up and he tried to swallow. "Where are the others?"

"The three that my client's *alleged* to have buried," the solicitor replied. "Last time I checked, he hadn't been found guilty of any crime."

The fat detective turned his lizard gaze on the lawyer. "We found him at the scene, *burying* one of them. The DNA of three *other* people has also been found in the boot of his car."

It didn't take a space traveller with an off-the-scale IQ to notice that these men so badly wanted to turn off the cameras and tape recorders and dispense with traditional justice. It took all their willpower just to keep the conversation civil.

"Where are the other bodies, Mr Stanley?" the second detective asked.

I stared past them for a few seconds, getting an eyeful of beige wall, until I realised that they were talking to me. I fixed my accusers with a stare that made them shuffle uncomfortably.

"The others are about forty feet back from the main footpath, about sixty feet away from a big house – I can't remember the door number."

My solicitor tried to interrupt but I silenced him with a wave of the hand. I wasn't Martin Stanley, so I had nothing to gain by hiding his victims and denying their families some peace of mind.

The fat detective smiled. "How many?"

Something within the host surfaced, a little bubble of anger from a portion of his mind that I hadn't yet occupied, and the desire to wipe the grin off the detective's face overwhelmed me. I dropped the full truth on my interviewer.

"Eight."

That did it. One cheesy smile gone in the time it took him to process the number.

"Eleven in total?"

I nodded.

The detectives held their breath and looked at each other, barely able to understand what they were hearing.

"Well, eleven in Whitewebbs Wood."

Both men paused and gazed at me through narrowed eyes. The fat detective picked up a glass of water and glugged the contents. He lowered the empty beaker to the desk and stared at it for a few seconds, before he raised his eyes to mine.

"Are you saying there's more?"

Martin Stanley started killing women when he was twenty-six years old. It began with a Russian girl, Natalya, who made the innocent mistake of visiting the printers where he worked.

She went in there in the hope of selling some handcrafted Russian matryoshka dolls – you know, those nested things, one inside the other – but all she got for her troubles was a sexual predator with an eye for his first kill. And his eye couldn't help but fall on her.

She was pretty, petite, blonde and shy, with big blue eyes that glanced down when she talked. Somehow, Stanley got the girl talking, in her broken, guttural way, about how she'd ended up in Teesside. He asked her about her friends, her living arrangements, and family ties. Not because he was interested in her, but because he wanted to know just how badly she would be missed. She told him that she had no friends and lived on her own. Her parents had died in a recent car crash and she'd settled in England using the inheritance money.

His excitement increased.

Natalya was friendless, rootless, and alone.

She was the one.

He tried to keep her talking, but she said she needed to leave, so that she could try and sell her wares to other businesses in the area. In a panic, Stanley promised to buy some from her, for his family, if she agreed to go out with him on a date that evening. He suggested that she bring her dolls along for the date, to keep for company. She gave him a perfect white smile that sent his blood lust soaring.

He picked her up that evening, as the evening sky turned from burnt amber to maroon. He parked his car out of view of witnesses, and hit the horn to get her attention. She got in the front passenger seat and gave him a shy smile. Then she opened the zipper of her handbag and gave him a flash of the Russian doll that lay inside. He laughed, and she laughed too, believing that she was in on the joke rather than the butt of it.

They went for a long drive onto the Yorkshire Moors, keeping to the back roads. The landscape looked strange at night. Tree branches reached for the sky like withered claws, and in the darkness the plants and shrubs had a metallic solidity and sharpness. Stanley pointed at peaks and valleys arbitrarily, and told her stories about imaginary landmarks, to take her mind off the fact that he was taking her ever further from the beaten track.

The longer he drove the stranger the landscape seemed to be. Houses looked as flat as card and the people resembled lifeless mannequins. Fields of crops seemed to sway of their own volition, regardless of wind direction. Stanley drove until he no longer recognised his surroundings, and looked for a place to make his move.

Eventually, he pulled off the road, into a layby that was shielded by a thick bank of shrubs and trees, and told her that he had cramp in his foot. When the she looked into the darkness that surrounded them, the girl began to feel afraid. She chewed at her fingernails and asked a continuous stream of questions in broken English and useless Russian, while Stanley massaged his foot and said the word *cramp* in a loud voice – as though increasing the volume would somehow bridge the gap in their understanding.

He told her that there was a pub nearby, a cosy place where they could enjoy drinks next to a roaring wood fire, but the girl wanted to go home. She was frightened and confused and looked around with nervous twitches of her head. Tears rolled down her cheeks, though she didn't dare make a sound. Stanley stroked the girl's hair and told her that it was fine; he would take her home.

Then he dragged her into the back of the car and raped her.

The act itself didn't take long, consisting of little more than a minute and a half of savage thrusting, but the exquisite tension of the moment made it seem so much longer. That's the funny thing about time – it's a malleable thing that expands and contracts around us. Moments of ecstasy, like the one Stanley experienced, stretch themselves as thin as an elastic band, until it feels like the very fabric of universe might snap at a moment's notice. Those final vinegar strokes, with his forehead pounding painfully against the cold passenger window, whilst the terrified girl squealed beneath him, seemed like an eternity.

When he came inside her, time snapped back to normal, and he lay back against the seat for a few moments of satisfaction, his chest heaving from the effort. But the satisfaction didn't last long.

He watched the shaking girl pick up her torn panties from the footwell and try to put them on. He'd ripped away the gusset in his frenzy, so that the underwear consisted of one big hole. When she attempted to put her clothes back on, she realised that they were ruined and began to cry.

Stanley told her to get out of the car. The girl looked at him through tear glazed eyes and pleaded for her life. Her pleas aroused him. He got hard again, and when the girl saw that her pleas weren't going to help her, she screamed and pushed the door open.

She wasn't fast enough. Stanley grabbed a handful of Natalya's hair and pulled her back. She wailed and sobbed and flailed her arms as he pushed her on her stomach and entered her again. Stanley whispered to her like a lover, demanding that she do the same, but the girl didn't understand. He attempted to kiss her, but she turned away, so that her face was in the dirt, and cried into the leaves that littered the ground.

When he finished the second time, Stanley felt no satisfaction, only a sense of emptiness, like staring into an abyss. The abyss stared back. Stanley didn't like what it had to show him and tried to turn away, but there was no avoiding from what was inside him. He realised that if he couldn't turn away from what he'd done he could at least bury it.

Natalya sat on the ground and attempted to straighten her torn dress. Tears ran down her face and occasionally a silent sob shook her body like a shiver. Stanley couldn't stand to look at it any longer. He saw a large rock on the ground and picked it up. It was heavy in his grasp, and had lots of sharp edges. He made sure that he had a good grip as he approached Natalya. She was unaware of his presence as she fussed and fiddled with various buttons and cried softly.

He brought the rock down, again and again and again, until there was nothing left but an awful mess of blood and hair and brain pulp. He gazed without admiration at his handiwork for a few seconds. He'd snuffed out what made this girl human, leaving behind nothing more than a flesh container.

She was an empty vessel that needed to be filled. Part of him understood her plight. He'd been empty for most of his life – devoid of feelings, of empathy, of anything that might be mistaken for joy – so he wanted to find a way to communicate that. In his own way, he felt closer to her than any other person in his life.

He took the doll from the girl's purse and thrust it inside her, pushing it in deep with his fingers. Now Natalya was a human matryoshka doll – a little secret for the pathologist to discover, if they ever found the body.

Stanley pulled a shovel from the boot of his car and dug a deep grave. He pushed the body into the hole and rapidly shovelled earth on top of it. He shovelled the excess dirt into the area around him and used a branch to flatten the ground and make it look natural.

When he woke the next morning, the air felt fresher, food tasted better, and the world seemed different. He replayed the events in his mind constantly, until they gradually lost their lustre and felt like nothing more than a vaguely remembered dream. His life felt like a flat monotone photocopy of reality, without colour, without vitality.

He wanted to feel alive again, but there was only one way to do that.

For the next few weeks, whenever there was a news report on the TV or radio, Stanley paid close attention, with fear tightening his innards until he could barely eat, and hoped that nobody would discover his secret. As the weeks passed into months, he realised that nobody missed the girl. She was just another lost soul.

It got easier after that. The fear faded, and victim after victim found their way into graves all around Yorkshire. He was always careful to ensure that they were the ones that others wouldn't miss. Hitchhikers, prostitutes, foreigners that looked like they were here illegally, it was easy for people to disappear, especially when he was careful. The graves were *always* deep; his kill kit was *always* at the ready. When the time was right, his preparation was tight.

He got through a lot of kills in three years.

When Stanley moved to London, it was ostensibly for the work, but in reality he wanted a larger pool of lost souls to choose from. It worked for a while (it was easy for people to disappear in the big city), but new relationships and maintaining friendships all got in the way, until he couldn't do what he wanted and his disguise (as a regular human being) became his main way of living.

So the killing stopped, but the rage continued to bubble beneath the surface: The urge to rape, kill, and wield power over those who were weaker than himself continued to percolate. It crippled him socially, financially, and it took a toll on his body. Comfort eating became his way of dealing with the problem; the more he wanted to kill the more food he ate. He grew fatter and more miserable with each passing day.

By the time he ended up in Enfield, Stanley was barely functioning as human being. When he looked at women on the street, he saw only victims, he imagined their screams, the terror twisting their pretty features, and most of all he fantasised about the moment when the life left their eyes. It was that moment that he missed most of all – the moment of death.

He bought a car, despite crushing debts, and cruised the streets for victims. He picked them off quickly, killed them sloppily – raping them fast, burying them shallow, leaving all kinds of evidence in his wake – and eventually paid the price of an uncomfortable seat in a beige interview room with two detectives.

I'll never forget the look on the fat detective's face when I gave him the final figure. It was a look of horror mixed with barely concealed delight. His lips were pressed tightly together, pursed in a look of thin-lipped anger that could just have easily been a smirk. His eyes were narrowed and mean on the surface, but far beneath, dancing somewhere in the jet back pupil, I could sense the struggle not to scream with joy. His horror at the ferocity and quantity of my crimes was plain to see, but his delight wasn't too hard to notice if you looked for it. Catching Martin Stanley made his career, you see. His name made the papers and the TV, thanks to the killer's blunders. Word on the lunatic's grapevine is that they've just given the man a promotion. Good for him.

I also remember the way his face fell when I told him what I actually was, and that Martin Stanley wasn't really there anymore. The light in his eyes faded just a little, because it meant a madhouse rather than prison.

They brought in the finest criminal psychologists, and then sent them away – bamboozled. They did MRIs and CAT scans, studying my amygdala for signs of aberrant behaviour. They tested my IQ, and found it to be 'off-the-charts', as one of them put it, despite the fact that previous tests put Stanley between 130-140. They prodded and poked and tested, only to find that my 'fantasy' was so deeply ingrained that they had no choice but to declare me insane.

The authorities hunted for bodies in all the places that I suggested and found them one-by-one.

But they couldn't find my first victim.

In my confusion, I suggested several alternative burial sites. Maybe Stanley had locked the knowledge so deep, behind layers of lies, that I had trouble discerning the truth. Everywhere they dug the result was the same. No corpse, no evidence of a corpse, and a lot of police officers left scratching their heads.

They put me in a room with a criminal psychologist. He was a pale, dark-haired man of indeterminate age in a black suit and white shirt combo. He had a prissy way of licking the tip of his pen before he wrote something on the clipboard he had in his lap. His beady blue eyes studied my face, twitching up and down and left and right for details that he could jot in his report. The man's lips were locked in a permanent smirk. I wasn't sure if this was a physical defect or an overwhelming contempt for yours truly – either way, it annoyed me.

"Do you know what I think, Martin?"

I smiled at him. "I wish you wouldn't call me that."

He tapped his left temple with the end of his pen. "Of course. So what *would* you like me to call you?"

"It's unpronounceable."

The psychologist cast a glance at the two guards, who shuffled and snickered softly. I glared at them. They returned my glower with interest, but my gaze darkened to such a degree that they turned and looked away.

I slouched in my chair and said: "The human tongue's incapable of generating the sounds required to pronounce it. It's a question of biology. You just don't have it."

"Maybe because that's the way you want it."

"No. It's just the way it is."

"Then how about I call you Mr Stanley?"

"I guess it'll do."

He propped his elbows on the clipboard and leaned forward. "Wormholes, alien worlds, body snatching, it's all very convenient."

"Not for me," I replied. "I'm trapped in this body."

"You could always end it."

"Is that an invitation?"

He smiled. "No, Mr Stanley, a hypothetical point."

"We're not allowed to endanger our hosts," I replied.

"Why?"

"We're not savages."

"And yet you're debating whether or not to end the human race."

"We're gathering evidence to determine how dangerous humanity is – there's a difference."

"Did you know that your amygdala function is almost non-existent when faced with images of horror that would make a normal person's scan light up like a Christmas decoration?"

"*His* amygdala function."

"No, Mr Stanley. *Yours.*"

I decided to not argue semantics with him. "Which proves what exactly?"

The psychologist's smirk intensified. "Nothing. It's just interesting, that's all." Then he used the pen to tap his temple again. "Has it ever occurred to you that the Russian girl and the dolls might've been an imaginary event?"

I shook my head. "No."

"Why?"

"Because the memory's too vivid to be a dream."

"Haven't you ever had a dream so real that when you wake you have to pinch yourself to remind you where you are?"

I often dreamed of my home world, and of those I'd left behind. "Maybe."

"There are no records of this girl *anywhere.* Not here, nor in Russia. Believe me, we checked."

I shook my head. "Means nothing. People disappear all the time. Russia's not exactly renowned for the detail of its records. After all, Stalin was responsible for more deaths than Hitler, yet it's not something that's widely recognised."

"And Chairman Mao was responsible for more deaths than both of them combined," the psychologist replied. "There's always a psychopath with a bigger kill count."

"That's beside the point."

"I know what your point is, Mr Stanley. You say she's not on the records... maybe because they're lost, or they're being held somewhere off the beaten track."

"Something like that."

"And my point is that maybe this was something you *wanted* to happen. A dream so lifelike that it convinced you that it was real."

"Bollocks."

"No, no, Mr Stanley. Sometimes we have dreams that we *believe* are real. Alien abductions, for instance, often stem from sleep paralysis. Did you know that?"

"No."

He jotted that down. "There's no convincing many of these people that what they experienced was in fact a sleep anomaly. This is despite the fact that many of them don't ever remember seeing their *abductors,* just a sense of isolation, of dislocation, and an inability to move. Their brains fill in the rest and make it seem real."

"So?"

"You wanted it to be real. A dream so vivid that you convinced yourself it *was* real. The girl was a figment of your imagination, but it laid the groundwork for what you are now."

[197]

Grinding my teeth from side-to-side, I glared at him and tried to think of something to say that would cut the meeting short.

"And her Russian tongue? The matryoshka doll? I made them up, too?"

"The doll's a metaphor."

"For what?"

"For you, Mr Stanley."

My eyes sought his. I tried to stare him down, make him blink and look away, but his gaze was unflinching.

"You've been hiding yourself for a long time. I doubt anybody could truly get to the bottom of you – I certainly can't. After all, you're the student who gambled during university and lied about it for years, shielding your debts from your family. You played the devoted boyfriend to numerous women, shielding them from your murderous instincts. You covered your tracks by creating a hard-drinking, gregarious persona, shielding your friends from the quiet, soulless predator you really are. You've been covering yourself in new layers for years. And this alien persona is simply the latest."

I felt cold, yet sweat dripped down my back and nestled unpleasantly in my waistband. "I know who I am. What I am."

"Do you?"

I tried glaring at him again, but his gaze was so intense and ferocious that I was the one who blinked and looked away.

"It's awfully convenient that you were possessed in mid-chase," he said. "Just as you realised the trouble you were in."

"This isn't a persona."

"I've got no doubts you believe that."

"I want to go back to my cell."

The man smiled. "Fine, but you can't avoid the truth. You have to face it eventually."

"I know what I am."

"A murderer."

I shook my head. "That's him, not me."

"It's *you*."

"You're wrong."

The man sighed and looked at my chaperones. "Take him back."

So here I am, sitting in the dark, quite alone. Nobody believes me, not even you. And why should they? After all, it sounds so outlandish. But we're everywhere, watching you all the time. It's not a lie.

That's why you should turn away for a few seconds and let me run.

I'm in charge now, not Stanley.

I'm in control.

I'm harmless.

I'm good.

I'm not a matryoshka doll.

There are no layers. Just me.

So open the door and let me go.

Hello, are you still there?

Twelve

I hear his muffled voice fade away as my feet take me further and further back from the door. The alien. He killed all of these women. He-
I'm surrendering to gravity as my heel thumps against the face of one of the corpses and gives my balance a jolt, toppling me backwards through the air. My arse splats down into the sticky lake of blood that coats the floor, and a ringing in my ears accompanies a harsh pain in the back of my skull as my head bounces off of the wall. I gasp in agony, bringing my hand up to check my head. For a split second I'm convinced that I've busted my skull open, but then I'm brought into the reality of the fact that I'm now caked in the gore of Martin Stanley's victims and the blood on my fingers isn't mine. I try to bring myself upright but my stupid shoes can't get any stupid purchase in the dark red liquid and I slip back, arse first into the gore. Still my ears ring that high pitched ethereal sound that's much like that old party trick when you run your finger around the rim of a wine glass.

"I don't belong here!" Martin Stanley roars from his room, but it doesn't really register properly behind the ringing. I find myself crawling on my hands and knees toward a door so that I can use the handle to drag me upright. The corpse of a woman stares up to me. The horror of Martin Stanley's actions still registering in her cold dead face. They used to say that a murder victim's eyes might still hold the image of their killer burned into their retina. From the look of her I would quite happily never see that image. Her arm is twisted so tight behind her back that I can see the lump of her dislocated shoulder popped out through the blue material of her scrubs. Her throat is torn open, like he started to cut off her head like he did with Amanda – Spark's plaything- and then gave it up. Maybe she was his last victim before he took himself off to bed. She's only young. A slender petite brunette with huge brown eyes. High cheekbones. Far too pretty to work in a place filled with psychotic men. Far too pretty to live, it would seem. Her skirt has ridden up to reveal no pants. She probably came to work with some on. Fucking Martin Stanley.

The closest door handle seems to get further and further away with every cold slap of my hands into the blood. The young nurse remains at my side. Her eyes boring into me. Accusing me. I should have been here to help her. But how could I be? How could I know? This was Benny's fault. Not mine. I didn't know she was here. I haven't had any training. I didn't even want this fucking job in the first place. Why did I apply? I don't remember applying. I don't even remember getting here anymore. So much shit has happened. I need to call the police. They need to know what's happening here. They need to know about this mysterious Dr Bracha, and Benny, and his psychotic twin.

Still the handle continues to elude me, and I've been crawling for about five minutes. Something's not right.

From beneath the blood something rises. A head. Benny. First his head, and then his shoulders, and torso. This isn't happening. He's laughing that same booming laugh that Gary spouted at me earlier. The dead girl twists. Her arm slides from beneath her and there's the sickening pop of her shoulder sliding back into place. She sits up, cross-legged beside Benny, who stands over me, still laughing. Between her legs I can see that she's wearing no underwear. I shouldn't stare but I do. She

[201]

looks up to him and blood spills from the gaping wound in her throat. He holds his hand out to her, rubbing his fingers together as if enticing a cat with invisible food, and waves his hand around. Her eye line follows him dutifully, until he waves his hand just a little too far behind her and the weight of her head forces it to drop back and there's the sound of tearing flesh and all I can see anymore is the open hole of the top of her neck. Benny laughs some more as he balls up his fist and begins to slide it deep into the girl's exposed oesophagus. He drops to his knees, and whilst he fist-fucks the open throat with one hand he pulls the other to his face, flicking his tongue between two outstretched fingers. I scream. I'm not proud of it, but I scream. This is fucked. I try to push myself back away from them but it's no use. The blood on the floor is too slippy. I can't bear this. My arms come up to my face to shield this sight from my vision. But the noise. Benny's laughter and the wet gargled bubble-pops of her neck spewing more blood around his elbow. My screams. Then nothing. Benny is gone. The girl is on the floor. Dead. In the same place as she always was. Me with my back to the wall, and a throbbing ache in the rear of my skull.

I'm up on my feet, stepping through the blood as carefully as I can whilst ripping the soaked shirt from my back. The blood has soaked through to my vest so I rip that from my body too, discarding my clothes to the floor, and scanning every door left in the corridor for anything that might provide a tap, or towels. Anything. The metallic stink of blood is everywhere, and I retch some more but it's seriously no use. I can't think of the last time I ate. What did I even have? This place is killing me.

Minutes later I find a staff toilet. Again the lighting is much crisper than anywhere else in this fucking building, so much so that it's almost startling. I make my way to the first sink of four and turn on both taps. From a dispenser on the wall I pull towel after towel and dunk handfuls into the water and I scrub at my skin. The diluted blood streams down my body, and through the masses of hair on my chest, back, and down over my swelled gut. I don't remember ever being *that* hairy. Or fat. But surely I must have been. What's happening to me? The pink water weaves its way between the hair, stopping to tug gently at each and every one of them, ticking me softly. Still I drag the sopping wet towels across my skin and try to clean the sticky awful blood away. Beside the sink the pile of red towels builds higher, the blood drips a tap tap tap onto the tiled floor. Then that familiar tip tap of the moth comes into my ear space. Whilst dragging handtowels across my waist I crane my neck to see it there. Again. The moth. My only company on this fucked up trip. It tip taps against the ceiling, heading for the light panel behind me. It tip taps gently, basking in the glow of the fresh and clean lighting of the bathroom. It tip taps just a little more, before I crush its tiny fucking body against the plastic with the end of a mop handle. Take that, Mr *fucking* moth. The insignificant corpse hangs on to the plastic casing of the light panel for just a few seconds with the glue of its innards, before it drops to the floor. Dead. I watch the black blob on the floor, and smile a satisfied grin. That's all it takes to snuff out a life. I'm reminded of Martin Stanley, and what he did to those girls. The way he ended their lives so quickly and without remorse. My smile drops from my face and I instantly regret my minor crime. It's not the same but it kind of *is.* I hover my shoe over the corpse of the moth and I slam it down, crushing its, what? Skeleton? My heel grinds from left to right, disintegrating the thing. Removing the evidence. I turn back to the sink and I want to reach out for more towels but I can't. I'm frozen. Because *he's* looking out at me. From the mirror. *Benny.* It's *his* gut I've got. *His* tits. *His* bulging fat cock protruding from beneath the drum-skin stretched grey trousers. That isn't me. It's *him.* This is a dream. Of course it is. It's the old cliché where I wake up and it was all some fucked up reverie. Fucking *Benny!*

Without a thought I rush toward the mirror. It takes all the will in the world not to raise my hands to stop myself from smashing my forehead into the mirror, which doesn't crack. There's just a dull thud as I bounce from the glass, and then I have a cracking ache not only at the back of my head but at the front too.

"Fuck's sake," I say through gritted teeth. I'll fuck Benny up before I wake up, so help me fucking God and his little lad Jesus. I charge forward again. This time the mirror cracks with the force, and several shards drop out under the irresistible force of gravity. The larger shard cracks again as it hits the sink, and becomes several blood stained shards. In the fractured reflection I see Benny's skull broken at the forehead. Blood streams down his face. I laugh. That same booming *Benny* laugh. The kind of laugh that says if I didn't then I would probably cry. I stagger toward the mirror once again, but this time I lift a shard out of the sink, and place the tip against my cheek. I feel no pain as I put a small amount of pressure on it and my cheek begins to tear. This will teach you for fucking with my head *Benny. Gary.* Whoever the fuck you are.

"Stop!" a voice calls out. There's nobody in here but me.

"Fuck you!" I call out, "fuck this fucking building, and fuck Dr fucking Bracha!"

"Dr Bracha's upstairs," says the voice, "you can talk to him any time. The same as I can."

"Who are you?" I ask, still holding the shard to my cheek.

"I'm Darren."

"*Where* are you?" I ask.

"I'm having a shit," he chuckles, "first thing I did when you let me out. Been here ages."

"When *I* let you out? I did no such thing." I say calmly.

"If you say so," he says, "you're almost ready to meet Dr Bracha," he says, "so shut your trap for just a minute will you? I've got a story for you."

Urban Paranoia

By Darren Sant

HOW DID I get here? Some might say it was an unfortunate series of events. Unkind folk would blame me entirely. The truth is I don't really know what made me do it. They've called me a paranoid, psychotic and dangerous person in the press. The relatives have called for them to throw away the key. I'll let you judge for yourselves.

June 1st

As my fingers flew over the keys with practised ease my head throbbed with the first stirrings of a headache. In my tiny little study a radio played a Pixies track and I smiled at memories of days gone by. A sudden loud crack drew my attention to the world outside my window. I looked out and saw a man throwing the "To let" sign from next door into the back of a van. So they'd finally managed to find tenants for the place ... nightmare scenarios of crazy neighbours quickly flashed through my mind and the pounding in my head increased in tempo.

June 2nd

I awoke with the cat nuzzling my face, her grey tail swishing with impatience.
"Alright, flea bag, I'm getting up."
She gave me the kind of look that left no doubt as to who was in charge here and what she would do in my slippers if I didn't do as I was told.

I climbed out of bed and wandered to the bathroom to take care of pressing business. After putting out the cat's food I opened the kitchen window and sighed happily at the sound of the birds. It promised to be a lovely day if the rain kept off.

I was sitting at the kitchen table enjoying coffee and toast when the thunderous roar of approaching apocalypse battered my ears. I walked through to the living room and looked out of the window. A blue Subaru with tacky yellow door panel stickers was half-blocking my drive. I could hear the thunderous roar of the exhaust as the driver unnecessarily pressed the accelerator pedal with the car in neutral. I heard the *thump thump* of bad techno pounding from two huge speakers mounted on the car's parcel shelf. The distortion hurt my ears even from a distance.

The cacophony stopped as a bald-headed man stepped from the car. A spider web tattoo covered half of his face and a Woodbine drooped from his mouth.

"Declan, Courtney – help your mum unpack the boot whilst I get the dog," he bellowed. The man threw his Woodbine into my drive and opened one of the car's back doors. A huge Rottweiler bounded from the back seat and immediately pissed up a bush at the end of my drive. It was quickly followed by two moody looking teens. The lad was dressed all in black, wearing boots that looked three sizes too big for him; he was so pale he looked like he shouldn't be out in the daylight. He was followed by a girl of about seventeen wearing shorts that almost weren't there. Her crop top revealed more than it should have, but she was oblivious to everything but her phone, to which her eyes were glued. The last person to emerge from the car was a clean-looking woman dressed plainly and prettily. She had the ghost of a smile and already I pitied her. She caught my eye through the window and I quickly retreated back to the kitchen to eat my toast and finish my coffee. My head started to pound with another headache as I contemplated my new neighbours.

June 3rd

I awoke with cold sweats and listened for the thunderstorm that had woken me up. The clock told me it was 2 a.m. I groaned and sat up in bed, blinking. I heard a steady rumble that I slowly realised was actually not outside, but coming through the wall behind my head, from the house next door. I listened closer and realised it was fucking dance music. At 2 a.m. on a Tuesday fucking morning. I groaned and put the pillow over my face and tried to sleep; my head started to throb in time with the music.

The noise had abated at around 4 a.m. and I'd had just a few hours of very broken sleep when I got up at 7 a.m. I showered and shaved and felt a little better as I got dressed for work. As I got into my car and reversed down the drive, I could see that my neighbours' car was still blocking my driveway. I reversed as far as I could and left the car idling as I walked over to their front door. I rang the bell and waited. After a minute or so there was still no sign of life so I rang it again, waited. Still nothing. I looked at my watch. If they didn't hurry it up I'd be late for work. I knocked on the door. Still nothing. I knocked louder. The dog started barking and I heard the door shudder as it hurled itself at it. Jesus Christ, that thing was fucking big.

The door was suddenly flung open and the big man held the dog by the collar as it barked and snarled at me.

"WHAT?" he yelled aggressively.

I took a step back.

"Listen, mate, I live next door and I've got to get to work and you're blocking my drive."

He looked over at where I was pointing at his Subaru. "Okay." He shut the door in my face and I once more heard the dog throwing itself at it.

I went back to my car and after ten minutes he came out and moved his car a few inches. Gave me just enough room to get out. The wanker. I wound down my window to mutter a sarcastic "thanks" but his back was already to me as he headed back to his house. I heard him mutter "ponce" loudly before shutting the door.

I barely functioned at work. Endless cups of coffee couldn't take away the tiredness from sleep deprivation. My now constant headache grew in intensity with my caffeine intake. At six o'clock I turned into my close and swore as I saw the Subaru once more blocking my drive. I drove right up to the car and left my ignition on. I got out, slamming the door behind me, and stomped up to their front door. I knocked loudly and was rewarded by the Hound of the fucking Baskervilles once more trying to smash through the door. The door was answered by the teenage girl who, I saw, was still clutching her phone.

"Yeah?"

"Can you ask your dad to move his car, please?"

She looked down at her phone and started typing.

"Hello." I waved my hand in front of her face. "Can-you-ask-your-dad-to-move-his-car-please."

I spoke slowly and sarcastically. She looked up from her phone.

"He's asleep."

"Well, bloody well wake him up, then. There's plenty of room in the street for his car that doesn't involve him blocking my drive."

"He gets mad when you wake him up."

I let out all of my anger in a huge frustrated sigh.

"Alright, alright. No problem. I'll knock for him later."

I considered that maybe he was the kind of bloke that would take out his anger on his family and I didn't want to be responsible for that.

I walked back towards my car, but before I made it I heard a yell.

"Bruiser! Get back here!"

I turned to see the dog streaking towards me and I ran the last couple of yards and shut the door just as the dog's face appeared at the window, its foam-flecked teeth pressing against the glass. My heart was pounding in my chest, I felt like I was going to have a heart attack. My head throbbed in time with it and I felt a sudden odd calmness come over me.

KILL IT a voice said from nowhere. I felt oddly disconnected from the world, all that I could focus on the voice. *KILL IT,* I heard again, like an echo.

"Bruiser, come here now!"

The dog took a last longing, hungry look at me before trotting back to the girl at the front door, its tail wagging like it wanted to play.

Once she'd gotten hold of the dog and given me a quick scowl, she closed the door. I parked up in the street and made my way into my house.

June 4th

I awoke with a headache. It wasn't helped by the yelling I heard from next door, punctuated by occasional loud barks. The cat gave me a quizzical look as she stared at the wall. She wasn't happy, either. I fed her and let her out, then wondered if I'd done the right thing by putting in a work from home day. I turned on the radio and was rewarded with a Zeppelin track. I cranked up the volume as I put the kettle on. Almost immediately I heard a banging on the wall and a yell.

"Turn it fucking down!"

I guiltily turned the volume down.

"You wanker!"

The room swam out of view and I staggered as a calm measured voice spoke to me. *KILL HIM FIRST*. I sat down at my kitchen table, hyperventilating and scared of what was happening to me. My hands shook as I tried to sip my coffee. I took deep calming breaths and tried to concentrate on the relaxation techniques my counsellor had shown me. I wouldn't allow these neighbours to give me another breakdown.

2:30 p.m.

I'd tried to forget the voice I'd heard and instead concentrated on work. I worked like a Trojan and finished spreadsheet after spreadsheet, firing them off to work and getting encouraging comments from my boss about my sudden surge in work rate. I refrained from calling him a smarmy wanker by return e-mail. The twat had more faces than Big Ben. A sudden commotion in the garden drew my attention. I dashed outside to see the cat arching her back and next door's dog advancing on her menacingly. I picked up a spade I'd left in the garden and hefted it over my head. *DO IT*. The cat suddenly turned tail and ran and was quickly up a tree in the corner of the garden. The dog gave chase, but it was way too slow for her. It snarled and barked at the bottom of my garden.

"Get out of my fucking garden before I stove your fucking head in, mutt."

The dog took one look at me and snarled. I walked forward, brandishing the shovel. It detected my lack of fear and eyeballed me. It skirted around me and ran down the drive, straight into its owner.

"Oi, Bruiser! Get here…"

The neighbour's voice tapered off as he saw me holding the shovel. *YOU COULD DO HIM NOW. NO ONE WOULD SEE.*

He pointed at me. "Touch that dog and I'll put you in the fucking ground, pal."

"Get it and yourself off my fucking drive."

I dropped the shovel with a load clang that made my neighbour flinch and walked back into my house; my heart was pounding in my chest. Ten minutes later the cat slunk back into the house and came to sit on my lap, where she dozed as I twitched and shook in fear and anxiety. What was happening to me?

That night as I lay in bed mulling over the day and trying to sleep I wondered if I should see the doctor about the voices. I guess that I must have drifted off; when I awoke it was to banging on the wall. A constant rhythmic thump, and this time it was not music. When I heard the first of the moans I knew what it was; the headboard, and her screaming for more under the sweating brute. She yelled loudly, begging to be fucked hard, and I sighed unhappily and stroked the cat, which lay asleep and twitching on the bed beside me.

It seemed to go on all night. I heard laughter, and music. My misery couldn't have been more palpable than if it sat in a chair staring morosely at me from the corner.

June 5th

I awoke once again feeling tired. My ever-present headache was starting to feel like an old friend now, I'd wonder what was wrong if I didn't have a headache. The cat slipped off the bed and slunk down the stairs to await her food. I blinked the sleep out of my eyes as I entered the bathroom.

Blood covered the room in small puddles. Thick congealing clumps slid down the tiles. Red viscous liquid ran overflowing from the toilet bowl and chunks of grey and pink matter floated in the sink. On the mirror above the sink, two words written in blood: KILL THEM.

I gasped in horror and covered my face, my heart pounding in my chest with fear and nausea. I looked again; nothing, the bathroom was clean.

I staggered down the stairs, gripping the banister with every step, my hands white-knuckled. I made it to the kitchen before I vomited into a sink full of dirty dishes.

At eight I called into work and pleaded a migraine so I could have the day off. I left the curtains drawn and switched on the TV. I immediately muted the sound and watched grey images wash over me without effort. I curled up into a foetal ball. I pressed "play" on the stereo remote and found a classical station. As soothing strains of harp and flute washed over me, I lay curled up. The cat tried to get my attention but gave up after a couple of impatient meows and slipped out of her cat flap to find her own breakfast.

I must have lain there for hours in the darkened room. The only noise I made was to laugh at the silent pantomime that was the Jeremy Kyle show on mute. As I watched some of the dregs of

[213]

society, a beautiful orchestra played from the radio and I laughed and laughed until I was hoarse and coughing.

Loud music from outside in the street had my eyes on stalks, flicking back and forth nervously. I crept to the curtains and looked through a small slit. A Citroen Saxo was blocking my drive. A guy wearing a Burberry cap stood beside it talking to my new neighbour. All the time the car's stereo pounded out a beat. Money exchanged hands and my neighbour handed over a small polythene bag containing god knows what. They didn't even have the good grace to look around furtively. *DO IT. THEY DESERVE IT*.

The Saxo driver climbed into his car and drove off with tyres squealing. My neighbour strutted back to his house. I looked to my fireplace, at the ceremonial sword that hung there. A gift from an old friend. The scabbard was finely crafted wood with elegant carving curving up the length of it. The blade was still razor sharp. I walked slowly over to it and with trembling hands lifted the sword from its stand. I withdrew the blade and flinched at the harsh rasp as it caught the brass trim on the edge of the scabbard. I let the scabbard fall to the floor with a loud thud and lay back down, quietly stroking the blade's flat side. As Mozart played, Loose Women came on the TV. I was oblivious to all.

June 6th

I awoke in the early hours, uncomfortable from sleeping on the sofa. The sword was on the floor; no doubt it had woken me up when it fell from my grasp. I blinked and the room was in darkness except for the glow of the TV, which displayed one word in blood red letters: MURDERER. I got up quickly, nearly tripping over the sword, and switched the TV off at the wall. The word glared back at me defiantly for half a minute before slowly fading away.

June 7th

I skipped work again; my head was throbbing. I'd taken to having a morning cocktail of paracetamol and Ibuprofen, but nothing shifted the headache completely. Nothing dulled the voices or my obsession with my neighbours. I'd often hold a glass up against the wall to hear them talking. I'd stand there for long minutes trying to catch a word or phrase. I lurked in the back bedroom with the sword in my hand, looking out over their garden, which was already overgrown and messy. Large dollops of dog shit sat like land mines waiting to be trodden on. The beast himself trotted up and down the garden, barking at anything that moved. I stared down at it with bloodshot eyes, caressing the hilt of the sword. All the time voices whispered *DO IT. DO IT*.

I was desperate to leave the house, but every time I walked down the drive my stomach knotted in fear and my headache worsened by degrees with every step.

The third time I tried, the young Goth lad from next door was sitting on the wall by my driveway with his mate, laughing and smoking joints; they threw the tab ends into my garden. They watched my faltering, hesitant steps and laughed as I headed shakily back to the house. I heard calls of "weirdo" and more laughter. *GET THE SWORD*. I shut the front door behind me and stood there gasping for breath with sweat rolling down my forehead.

June 10th – Judgement Day

I awoke from a fitful, nightmarish sleep to a god-awful row. I looked out of the window. A street lamp cast an insipid glow over a terrible event. Next door's dog had something in its mouth and was shaking it vigorously on my front lawn. I ran down the stairs and out of the house. The dog looked at me defiantly and dropped its prize before running back next door and around the side of the house.

I sank to my knees and held the near lifeless grey thing in my arms. The cat looked up at me and meowed weakly before her eyes closed for good. I looked up with tears streaming down my face and saw that bastard from next door smirking down at me before he closed his curtains. I carried the cat gently – as if I could hurt her now – and laid her down on the back lawn. I went to my garage and returned with a shovel. I dug a shallow hole and buried her. I worked like an automaton, no feelings, just numb and never stopping for a breather. The voices in my head were working overtime. *NO GOING BACK. NOW IS THE TIME*. With the job finished, I returned to the house and grabbed something I'd need, then walked calmly around to next door and knocked on the door. I continued knocking without stopping until someone answered.

The bully yanked the door open and eye balled me. "What do you want, you fat fuck? Do you know what time it is?"

I brought the sword from behind my back and rammed it through his chest. Blood bubbled from his mouth and his eyes widened in surprise and shock. I twisted the sword through three hundred and sixty degrees to cause maximum pain as I slowly withdrew it. Blood spattered everywhere as the sword slid from his body with a fleshy pop. He slid to the floor and I stabbed down too many times to count. I sliced and I poked and I prodded until what had once been a man was a load of bloody, hacked meat on the floor before me. A blood-curdling scream made me look up; his wife was on the stairs. When she saw me look at her she ran back up the stairs and I heard a door slam. I barely registered her existence.

I stepped out through the door and walked around the side of the house to the back garden. There I saw my goal: the kennel of the beast that had slipped its chain and left the garden after a careless scumbag had left the garden gate open. I advanced upon the kennel. A pair of yellow eyes regarded me with interest and not a little malice. I strode forward purposefully, leaving a bloody trail behind me. The beast must have known my intention, as it flew from the kennel and leapt at me. We went down together. The dog was going for my throat, but I batted it off with the sword; it yelled as I sliced its side. Still it fought with power and I let the sword drop and grabbed it bodily, and with all my might forced it off me. It came at me again immediately, but I'd grabbed the sword again by then and I held it out. The attacking dog impaled itself on the razor sharp blade. I push it further in and stood my ground, albeit a little shakily. I withdrew the sword and the dog yelped in pain. It was over; I slashed and hacked.

When the armed response unit turned up I was oblivious to them. I was busy decorating the bushes with the dog's intestines. I marvelled at the patterns the reds and pinks made draped over the bushes. I'd used most of the dog's organs and some limbs to spell out REVENGE on the patio.

I never heard the first warning or the second. I just felt white hot agony as a Taser blasted thousands of volts into me. I reckon if I'd still been holding the sword, they'd have shot me. When I passed out it was a blessed relief to be free of that single voice in my head that said *KILL KILL KILL KILL KILL KILL KILL*.

***

So you see, I was driven to it. It wasn't my fault. You'd have done the same thing, right? You want to know the real killer, the punchline? I have a fucking brain tumour. The part of the brain it's in means that it is inoperable. It caused the voices and the headaches and the doctor tells me I might have months and yes, it was no doubt a contributory factor in my behaviour, but society can't forgive what I did. I cast a glance at the empty, padded room that surrounds me. Small mercy, but I suppose I'd rather die in here than in prison. At least it's quiet. A whisper ricochets around inside my skull: *KILL*.

Mostly quiet, anyway.

Thirteen

"What the fuck has that got to do with anything?" I cry out from my curled up position on the tiled floor. The blood that pours down from my forehead stings my eyes and the world hides behind a rose tint. Not *that* kind of rose tint.

"Everybody's here for a reason, Ryan," says Darren from the toilet, "that much is for sure," he says, "we all have our stories. Our tales to tell."

"So? What's that got to do with me? I'm just a night guard."

Hysterical laughter resonates around the bathroom.

"Oh aye, pal, you keep telling yourself that, then you'll never meet *Dr Bracha*. We'll all be stuck in here forever."

I frown, and pull myself upright, staggering toward the toilet stall. I make a solid point of avoiding the mirror.

"What do you mean?" I ask of the door.

"I can't tell you, Ryan. You need to figure it out for yourself."

"Who's Ryan?"

The man in the toilet stall sighs impatiently. Says nothing. Pulls a couple of revolutions' worth of bog roll from the dispenser, scrunches it up and wipes his arse.

"Who the fuck is Ryan?" I ask, a little more urgently. Still he says nothing and takes another go at wiping his behind. I slam my hand against the toilet door.

"Answer me, for fuck's sake!"

The toilet flushes. The door opens to reveal a well-built bloke, a sneering grin behind his glasses. The harsh light of the bathroom shimmers in a sweating reflection from his bald head. He looks pointedly at me, expecting me to get out of his way, but I don't. We awkwardly stare at one another for a few seconds, and eventually he sniffs, pushing his glasses further back along his nose.

"You are," he says, "you're Ryan Bracha. Today. Tomorrow you might be somebody else."

He shoulders past me into the less confined space of the rest of the bathroom. I stare into the cubicle that he's just come from, a musky turd aroma weaves its stinking way up into my nostrils, and a thought about what the hell the bloke's diet is like threatens to disturb my blank mind. The man, Darren, pushes twice against the liquid soap dispenser. I'm *not* Ryan Bracha.

"Last week, you punched Richard Godwin in the face," he says, "because he told you about the porcupines."

"I didn't. I've never met Richard Godwin," I say. And I haven't. He wouldn't let me in.

Darren pushes down onto the tap to release the hot water.

"You have. Many times," he says, "I shouldn't be telling you this. You're supposed to figure it out yourself," he says, "or else you'll never get fixed."

"What do you mean? Fixed of what?"

He brings a dripping hand up from beneath the water and prods it against his temple.

"Fixed in the head," he says, looking at me through the mirror. Still Benny stands in my place behind his reflection.

But I'm just the guard," I say, my tone hints less at anger and more at confusion.

"Oh aye, the guard routine. We've all had it. It doesn't work but they insist on keeping it up. Okay, tell me this. How did you get here today?"

I can't answer his question. I don't remember. My eyes search the back of my mind for some distant memory of how I came to be at St David's but it eludes me. Darren smiles a smug grin, and continues to run the hot water over his hands.

"You were always here," he sneers, "I love it when he puts the new ones under like this. It keeps them from knocking the shit out of us all. Or worse."

"Under like what?"

"Confusion therapy," he says, "like Gary told you. It's what *he* does to the new ones. He tried to tell you anyway, but you were having none of it."

"How do you know about-"

"We *all* know, except you. We've all been through the same thing. We all got to the end intact, but still fucked in the head. You insist on fighting it. Keeping up the pretence that you're a normal bloke with a normal job to do. I'll tell you now, you *aren't* normal. Far from it, pal. You're a fuckin' psycho. He wouldn't have brought you here if you weren't. It's all he knows."

"I'm not. I'm-"

"A guard, I know, you said."

He pulls some towels from the wall and buries his hands into them. Drying off. Darren turns to me from the sink, dropping the towels to the floor.

"Look, you're boring me now, I need to go back to my room, and it's almost time."

"Time for what?" I cry out, this whole charade is fucking with my melon. Why does no cunt give a straight answer? I already know the reason, it's because they're all fucking lunatics. Darren sighs loudly.

"You'll never get it on your own will you?" he says, "Dr Bracha, upstairs. Figure it out."

"I can't, I don't-"

He prods a finger against his temple once.

"Up," he says, prodding again, "fucking," and again, "stairs."

He means in my head. He can go fuck himself. He's talking shit. Trying to mess with me. I launch myself at him, my fist connects really well with his nose. The man crumples to the floor, both hands up to his face. He starts to ask me what I'm doing but I'm on top of him, my knees pinning his shoulders to the ground, and I lay fist after fist into his mind-fucking face. He's crying, begging for me to stop but I can't. A particularly hard punch embeds the lens of one of his glasses into his eye, cutting the skin around it. Another punch bursts the eyeball behind the glass, and a disgusting jelly squelches out from beneath it, and over his cheek. Still the punches rain down, until he stops crying. Stops breathing. Stops living. I gaze down at the broken mess between my knees. The only sounds in this bathroom now are my heavy panting gasps, and the sticky drips of the blood pouring from his face. I drag myself upright using the sink, and I stare deep into the eyes on the man in the mirror. Something stirs inside me. A memory. The violence I've just inflicted upon Darren Sant triggered it. Fighting. The rush of adrenalin. I don't feel remorse. I feel alive. I feel excited. I want more.

The bathroom door is almost ripped from its hinges as I stride through it. My fingers already searching for the key. If what he said is true. If this is confusion therapy then there are no consequences to my actions. None of this is real. If that is true. Fuck it. If it's not, then I'll have some fun getting revenge on this fucking building.

The door swings open to reveal him.
"What are you doing? Why did you kill Darren? He won't be happy with you. He'll lock you away, like he did me," says Martin Stanley, the alien. The murderer. It's pretty much all he gets to say as I beat his last breath from his body. In what I'd take to be some sort

of ironic punishment I place my feet on the shoulders of his corpse as I place my arse on the floor, and I pull hard, and harder still against his head, until I rip it from his shoulders. Surprisingly it comes away with ease, and as I carry it by the hair I leave his room, leaving the body to pump blood all over the bed.

Still holding Martin Stanley's head by the hair I stalk along the corridor, stepping over the bodies of the women he killed, until I reach Gareth Spark's room. At the sound of the key in the lock I can hear him against the door. Tapping and asking to be released. Oh, you'll get your release Gareth. The door swings open and he attempts to leave the room, much like a cat trying to slink through the tiny gap, but I halt him by swinging the skull of Martin Stanley straight into his. The dull heavy thud of bone on bone sounds nice. Gareth Spark falls to the floor and I rain down blow after blow with the skull of my victim. The thuds turn to splats, and neither the skull in my hand, or the one attached to Gareth Spark's neck hold much by the way of solidity by the time I'm through.

I leave the room, my bare skin soaked in blood. Other people's, and my own. At the stairs I'm faced with two options, and one of them is drawing me a lot stronger than the other. I can go downstairs and end the lives of every single man down there. It's not real, after all. I can go and satiate my bloodlust. Or. Or I can go upstairs. I can find Dr Bracha, and end this once for all. End *him.* A buzz draws my attention above my head. A camera. The lens constricts. Zooms in. On me. This fucking place.

Before I know it I'm upstairs. I don't remember climbing the stairs, but I barely even remember pounding Darren Sant's face to a pulp either, so I don't worry about it. The door opens before I even touch it, and I'm in the corridor. It's even cleaner still here. Like the whole building is filled with shit, and the higher you go the cleaner and more clinical it gets. The first door I see bears his name. *Dr Ryan Bracha*. Darren Sant was talking shit about it being upstairs in my head. I'm standing right in front of physical evidence that he was talking bullshit. My hand moves as if to knock, but I overrule it this time. This bloke is getting fuck all by the way of etiquette. I want answers.

The door swings open to reveal an empty room. A desk with nobody behind it. A couch with nobody on it. And bed with nobody in it.

"Hello?" I call out to nobody. There's no answer. Of course there isn't. "Dr Bracha?"

I glide into the room, and take my time to look around. There's a white book case, filled with row upon row of paperbacks by people whose names I know, but they shouldn't be there. I scan my eyes across the books arranged in alphabetical order. I see Guns of Brixton by Paul D Brazill, through Fireproof by Gerard Brennan, and Mr Glamour by Richard Godwin on to dEaDINBURGH by Mark Wilson. On the desk is The Eagle's Shadow by Keith Nixon. I don't get it.

"I see you found his collection," says a voice which startles me into spinning around on my heels. Benny.

"You?" I say, but it's all I've got left in me, I have no other words.

"No mate," he says, "you."

"..."

"We're all you," he says, "or, I suppose more specifically, we're all Ryan Bracha. You're just one of us. The latest in a long line of fucked up characters he invents."

I don't say anything, but I feel the atmosphere in the room thicken, and suffocate me. An overwhelming nausea rides into my body like on the crest of a wave. The lights go dark, and I'm falling.

The First Sign

By Ryan Bracha

MADNESS is a funny thing. To those who do not suffer it, it is an aspirational condition, in the social sense. *I don't need any drugs to have a good time,* somebody might declare, *I'm mad enough as it is!* The man who is the life and soul of the party will forever be dubbed as mad as a term of endearment. The eccentric old woman in the run down house at the end of the street deemed *mad as a bag of snakes/box of frogs,* delete as appropriate. Madness is bandied about by idiots in a throwaway fashion because they'll never know true madness. Not like the men in here. Inside my head. Upstairs with *Dr Bracha*. The various manifestations of insanity. Like Brazill and his casual cannibalism. Furchtenicht's latent psychosis brought on by a sex mad dog. Godwin and his *porcupines* and rapist clones. Nixon and the case of the murdered woman. Wilson. Or Mary. Whatever you want to call them. Allen Miles' psychotic hatred of all things banal. Les Edgerton who sees fictional characters that guide him through life. Gerard Brennan, the dope smoking paranoid fitness freak. Spark, and his hallucinations. Stanley, *the alien.* And Sant. The neighbour from hell, depending on your viewpoint. Madness. It manifests itself in many ways. What's the worst? Me. Ryan Bracha.

I displayed the first signs of madness when I was fifteen. Aggression, emotional instability, paranoia. My parents, bless them, they put it down to a delayed response to a puberty I first hit at the age of ten. Sideburns at the age of twelve. A beard and six feet tall by fourteen. They pretended my behaviour was normal. The hallucinations came soon after. One time, I saw flames shoot out of my cock. That's the only explanation I have for why my grandfather's house burned to the ground, with him in it. I only just survived myself. It was the flames from my cock. I saw them, but I couldn't tell anybody. I told them I was asleep when the fire started. The police didn't believe me, I *know* they didn't. They sniffed around, asking questions, laying the blame of my grandfather's death at *my* door. It wasn't my fault. It was the cock-flames. How are you supposed to control them?

When I hit twenty I regularly got into fights, just for fun. I intentionally picked them with men twice my size. I enjoyed the feeling of my torso being pummelled for just the right amount of time before my anger would swell to uncontrollable levels and I would pulp their faces with my fists. I took their teeth as mementoes. One man I remember I punched so hard his eyeball burst against my knuckles as the socket cracked down the middle. That felt nice, it truly did. In those days we weren't monitored twenty four seven by the men in their CCTV control rooms. As long as you made a hasty enough getaway then you were okay. Just wash your fists. Your clothes. Hide the teeth. The evidence.

At twenty two I killed my first girlfriend. She's wasn't my *first* girlfriend, but she was the first one I killed. She'd been seeing people behind my back. I'd heard the rumours. There was the most prominent one in my mind about the time she went back to a party with five of my mates, and she took her time to go around and fuck each and every one of them in various rooms, including two of them at the same time. I smashed her face in with an iron. The appliance, not the golf club. I hid her corpse in the attic, bound up nice and tight with bubble wrap. She was a common slut. The five friends also went the same way over time. One in front of a train, another over a bridge into the swirling unforgiving frothy water of the river below. I have a good memory. I never forget.

Of course, the police would sniff around, asking their questions, making their insinuations. How could so many people I knew just disappear? At the time I made a pretty convincing show of being shit scared that I'd be next. I almost believed myself. They'd go away, content with my act, but then they'd be back. Where were you between the hours of whenever and whenever? Can anybody back you up to that effect? You do not have to say anything but if you do we're going to use it against you in court. But they had no evidence. Nothing. They had assumption, and they had a gut feeling. The assumptions and gut feelings were right, but hey ho, they had no evidence. They watched me. They had me under twenty four hour surveillance, but then they'd get bored of watching me live my normal life, and they'd go. And then I'd kill again.

My second girlfriend that I killed, well she wasn't exactly *my* girlfriend. She was somebody else's wife. She came to me through loneliness in a loveless marriage. That was fine by me. You see, another sign of madness is that detachment from reality, a distinct lack of emotional connection. She could flit in and out of my life, back to her cold bed, when we were done fucking each other's brains out. But, the thing was that her husband found out. He came to my door. Shouting his mouth off. Prodding my chest. Twice, I allowed him to prod, before I ripped off his finger, and jammed the thing into his ocular cavity. Of course, he cried and he screamed, until I dragged him into the house and strangled him dead. The girlfriend, whose name- despite my claims of a good memory –eludes me, showed up. She was worried that he'd done something stupid. She hadn't seen him in days. I confessed my crime to her, under some delusion that she would thank me for it. She didn't. In her eyes I could see fear, and terror. Her last word to me, beneath the cloud of fear, and with my fingers snaking around her neck, was *psycho*.

That was back, maybe seven or eight years ago. Before I came here. St David's. I'll get to the hows and whys soon. I just want you to see what I am.

Queuing for things. It was the very bane of my existence. Waiting. Wasting my life. Not a day would pass where I didn't bore holes into the backs of the heads of the people in front of me. Not literally, just with my eyes. Okay, so just once I literally did it, and I did at least show the initiative of waiting until I was out of the queue for the cash machine before I did it. But that's beside the point. My point, is that when I queued, I could feel myself drifting up out of my body, my itching fingers just slightly too eager to wrap themselves around a throat. That detachment again. That lack of concern for the well-being of others. As long as I was okay, then to hell with everybody else. I'm much the same now, but I'm *trying* to get better. I'm *trying* to become a better person. That's why I'm here.

There was a point in my life, at around the age of twenty nine, that I took stock. I'd murdered countless people throughout my time on Earth. People who I'd made claims to have loved at various junctures, but no sooner than I'd killed them I'd moved on, emotionally speaking. I couldn't form

[229]

relationships that meant anything. My approach to people was definitely more *Out of sight, out of mind,* than *Absence makes the heart grow fonder.* If you died tomorrow, I would forget you existed by the day after. It's just how I'm made, I can't fix that, but I'm trying. I promise you. I digress.

When I took that aforementioned stock of my life, I realised that time was the only thing between the present, and my inevitable incarceration. There was no if, only when. So I made a plan. I needed to get away from people. I needed to get out of society, because not only would I continue to slowly chip away at the population, but it would also slowly chip away at my mask. My public persona of somebody *normal.* But that age old question would rear its ugly head. What's normal? How do you become it? Does it even exist? All the people claiming to be mad, that they didn't needs drugs because they were mad enough as it was. *They* were the normal ones clamouring to be anything but, and I just had this voice inside me. Not the one that told me to kill people, that one was a booming loudspeaker. No, I mean the small voice that would sometimes creak through the cacophony of death, the one you could maybe stamp with the label of guilt, that one would beg me to become normal. To stop with the murder. The violence.

Eventually that voice grew stronger. With time. It learned to stand on its own two feet and halt me in my actions.

When I was twenty nine, I found myself standing over the unconscious body of a man. He had been in the process of burgling my house. Or at least trying to. I came downstairs to find him hanging into the open window of my kitchen. His legs on the outside, his torso in. I dragged him into my house and

I beat him senseless, and as I looked down at his broken body, I felt something. I couldn't truly say what it was, but it stunned me. This piece of shit that wanted to take what was mine for his own profit, he broke me. I sat on my sofa next to his gently breathing unconscious body, and I began to cry. That voice soothed me, and held off the screaming banshee that demanded I take his life.

I left the house that same night, and I walked. I walked until my feet bled, until my body gave in. I slept in a soft, and cold bed of heather along the Yorkshire moors. It wasn't a deep sleep, far from it. It was more a fitful and broken bout of nightmares, and half sleep. The boy from my house walked with me to Hell. At the gates of Hell he asked me a question. *Who are you?* I couldn't answer him. I didn't know. I was still a child. A lost and confused child, awaiting the time where I would awake from whatever nightmare I was living and I would be a fully functioning, *normal,* adult. That time never came.

In the morning I continued to walk along the road in the moors. Cars would scream by me , horns blazing out, warning me from the road. But they never stopped. Would you? A man covered in the dried blood of somebody else, in the road along the barren wilderness of the moorlands? I doubt it.

As the morning slipped quickly by and evolved into the afternoon I came across a derelict building. It hinted at a grand past. The huge architecture, once beautiful and revered, now gone to shit. The sign from the narrow dirt track which led up to the gates of the building, said *St. David's Asylum for the Criminally Insane.* At the time I saw it as in some way ironic, given that my own head was a minefield of disease. Now, at this time, after five years, I know it was fate.

The electricity supply was long gone, but the water supply remained. How long the building had been derelict I couldn't say, but it was, and that was important. I couldn't live in the society that began mere miles from the building. I couldn't bring myself to walk amongst civilisation. I was too dangerous for it. I would suffocate it one victim at a time.

Days, and weeks passed, and I busied my mind with small renovation tasks. Things like starting a vegetable patch. Or cleaning down the walls. Occasionally my mind would create the ghosts of lunatics from days gone by, but ghosts don't exist. I know this. You know this. It was my fucked up head trying to play tricks on me, but I was way too smart for that. I let the ghosts wander through me. I ignored them. I continued my life alone. But I was lonely. I began to create alter egos. People who could take over the shell that I'd become for a while, to allow my busy mind some sort of respite. I would give them back stories. I created Paul Brazill first. In my head he was an ex pat living in Poland, teaching English as a foreign language. He entertained himself by writing. That's what all of my alter egos had in common. They wrote. They had imaginations. They knew how to use them. I was so conceited that I wouldn't allow any of my *others* to be idiots. Then there was the Yank, Craig Furchtenicht. Then Godwin. They all lived in some degree of harmony amongst one another up in the prison that was my illness. Until I created Martin Stanley. He upset everything. He was a northerner, a graphic designer by trade, and he swept in, claiming to be an alien, and he wanted to take me away from the comfort of St David's. He wanted us to go into the nearest village and have us murder again. It affected the balance in my head. Upstairs. From then I had to lock them away. I was Benny, and Gary. Strolling the halls, harassing my *others.* They needed to be controlled.

And now my latest one. The new guard. He's tenacious, I'll give him that. But he needs to be controlled like the rest of them. He needs to know his place. He refuses to accept his role in this whole game. Already he's killed three of my *others.* Admittedly, Martin Stanley is no big loss. He is a liability, the nurses he removed from the bigger picture were no great loss, I can dream up more, but Darren and Gareth, I had really grown to like them. They entertained me. If this goes on there will be only me, and him. And I can promise you, if it comes to that, then, well, there will be only one outcome. And if I find myself alone again, after all this time, I cannot be held responsible for my actions.

Fourteen

I wake up. The room around me is small. The mattress beneath me is thin and stinks of piss. My piss? I don't feel any kind of cold around my crotch, but my hand reaches down regardless. Or at least it tries to reach down. I won't budge. I'm chained to the bed.

"What the fuck?" I ask of nobody, "what's happening?"

"Fuckin' dog!" a voice calls out. Furchtenicht.

"Craig?" I shout.

"Hey, fuck you newbie!" he replies.

"What's going on?" I ask.

"They moved Brazill upstairs and gave you his fuckin' room, asshole!" He then mutters something but he's too far away for me to make out.

Keith screams.

"Hey, Fruity Farts!" shouts a Scottish voice, Wilson, "stop yer greetin' ye wee fanny, ye'll see yer wee boyfriend again at dinner time!"

"Fuck you Wilson!"

Wilson, or Paul, laughs harshly into the corridor.

Keith screams.

"Shut the fuck up Keith!"

"Benny?" I call out to the heavy footsteps that clack along the hall. They pause, then clack my way. Stopping behind the door. A jangle. A click. The door opens.

"Alright there?" he smirks.

"What's happening? I don't belong here!" I cry.

"Neither do any of us!" laughs Allen Miles from his own prison.

"Boss' orders I'm afraid, you can't be trusted," he says, "you can't just go around killing his creations."

"What?"

"He needs them. To stay sane."

"I don't understand."

"Well, I reckon if you don't get it by now, you probably never will."

And he steps backwards, out of the room. Closing the darkness, and my screams, away, until another time.

THE END

Afterword and Acknowledgements

So it's finished. I can't believe that twelve weeks ago I asked eleven extremely talented chaps to get involved in this project, and we did it with ease.

Thanks must go then, to the eleven other mad men. You know their names but I'll name them again. Thanks to Paul Brazill, Gerard Brennan, Les Edgerton, Craig Furchtenicht, Richard Godwin, Allen Miles, Keith Nixon, Darren Sant, Gareth Spark, Martin Stanley and Mark Wilson. You made me really proud to be an indie writer.

Thanks again go to my wife Rebecca, for listening to me harp on about this project for the last three months. Thanks also for carrying our first and brand new daughter for the last nine months. I can't wait to meet her.

Thanks to the people that read and review not just my stuff, but the stuff of every indie writer out there. This book is a love letter to every other author out there that's trying to do something different with their work. Those of us that are willing to take a risk and put something new out there, you are my heroes, each and every one of you.

And thanks to the charities who will receive every penny of the profits from this book, for the hard and good work you do on a daily basis.

Much love to you all.

Ryan Bracha

Ryan Bracha is 34 years' worth of ideas just screaming to be unleashed on an unsuspecting public. By 24 he had written and directed his first feature film "Tales From Nowhere" which was well received and enjoyed a limited release around his native Yorkshire, his second screenplay "Dirt Merchants" never made it to screen but was an outlet for his desire to tell stories. Almost 4 years in the making, his debut novel, "Strangers Are Just Friends You Haven't Killed Yet" is a darkly comic satire based on the state of the media in the face of what appears to be a serial killer stalking the streets of Sheffield. It was the first of several number one ranking books, including his second novel, Tomorrow's Chip Paper, a gross-out collection of shorts the wonderfully titled 'Bogies, and other equally messed up tales of love, lust, drugs and grandad porn', and his critically acclaimed third novel, the semi-dystopian satirical thriller 'Paul Carter is a Dead Man'. Twelve Mad Men is his brainchild, and will hopefully be the first of many annual collaborative novels

Paul D Brazill

I was born in England and am now on the lam in Poland. I left school at sixteen and my first job was on a government scheme updating Ordinance Survey Maps. It wasn't as glamorous as it sounds. I've worked in a second-hand record shop and played bass in a couple of post-punk bands. I've been EFL teaching for over ten years and still seem to be getting away with it.

I'm the author of A Case Of Noir, Guns Of Brixton, Roman Dalton- Werewolf PI and a few other tasty snacks that you can find here.

My writing has quite shockingly been translated into Italian, Polish and Slovene. I know! I've had stories published in various magazines and anthologies, including The Mammoth Book Of Best British Crime 8, 10 and 11 - alongside the likes of Lee Child, Ian Rankin and Neil Gaiman. Which is nice.

I also edited the charity anthology True Brit Grit, along with Luca Veste, and a couple of other things, too.

Gerard Brennan

Gerard Brennan's short stories have appeared in numerous anthologies, including three volumes of The Mammoth Book of Best British Crime. He co-edited Requiems for the Departed, a collection of crime fiction based on Irish myths, and co-wrote The Sweety Bottle, a stage play. His novella, <u>The Point</u>, was published by Pulp Press in October 2011 and won the 2012 Spinetingler Award. Blasted Heath published his debut novel, <u>WEE ROCKETS</u>, in 2012, and they will release his latest novel, UNDERCOVER, in 2014. He is currently working on a creative writing PhD at Queen's University Belfast.

Les Edgerton

Les Edgerton is a full-time writer and writing teacher.

His work has been nominated for or won: the Pushcart Prize, O. Henry Award, PEN/Faulkner Award, Derringer Award, Spinetingler Magazine Thriller of the Year (Legends category), Jesse Jones Book Award, Edgar Allan Poe Award (short story category), Violet Crown Book Award, Nicholl's Foundation Script-writing Award, Best of Austin and Writer's Guild's screenwriting awards, and others. His 18th book, a black comedy crime caper, titled THE GENUINE, IMITATION, PLASTIC KIDNAPPING comes out in October from Down & Out Books.

Edgerton is an ex-con, having served two years at Pendleton Reformatory on a 2-5 sentence plea-bargained down for burglary, armed robbery, strong-arm robbery and possession with intent to deal.

Craig Furchtenicht

Craig Furchtenicht lives in rural Iowa, where many of his stories take place. His work generally spans the realm between drug-fuelled crime novels, short horror and the absurd. When he is not putting the words floating around in his brain to paper he enjoys cheering on his beloved Hawkeyes and spending time outdoors.

His works of fiction are the fantastic novel <u>Dimebag Bandits</u>, as well as the collections <u>The Blue Dress Paradigm</u>, and <u>Night Speed Zero</u>.

Richard Godwin

Richard Godwin is the author of critically acclaimed novels <u>Apostle Rising</u>, <u>Mr. Glamour</u>, <u>One Lost Summer</u>, <u>Noir City</u> and Confessions Of A Hit Man.

He is also a published poet and a produced playwright. His stories have been published in over 34 anthologies, among them The Mammoth Book Of Best British Crime and The Mammoth Book Of Best British Mystery, as well as his anthology of stories, Piquant: Tales Of The Mustard Man, published by Pulp Metal Fiction in February 2012.

Richard Godwin was born in London and obtained a BA and MA in English and American Literature from King's College London, where he also lectured.

You can find out more about him at his website www.richardgodwin.net , where you can also read his Chin Wags At The Slaughterhouse, his highly popular and unusual interviews with other authors.

Allen Miles

Allen Miles is a six foot three caffeine-addicted stick insect with a bit of a cold who lives in Hull and is twenty-nine years and thirty-four months old. He survives on three hours sleep a night and drinks far too much wine. His first major work, 18 Days, which peaked at #1 on the literary fiction chart, can be downloaded from Amazon and he is the co-proprietor of sittingontheswings.com.

His spare time is generally spent attention-seeking on various social media platforms and the release of his collection of novellas and short stories, This Is How You Disappear, is due later in 2014. Mr Miles is married with a three year-old daughter.

Keith Nixon

Keith Nixon has been writing since he was a child. In fact some of his friends (& his wife) say he's never really grown up. Keith is currently gainfully employed in a senior sales role meaning he gets to use his one skill, talking. Keith writes crime and historical fiction novels. His works of fiction are <u>The Fix</u>, The Konstantin Novellas, and <u>The Eagle's Shadow</u>. He is published by Caffeine Nights.

Keith also reviews books for Crime Fiction Lover and Al's Books & Pals blog.

Find him on Twittter (@knntom), Facebook, his blog (keithnixonauthor@blogspot.com) and Goodreads.

Darren Sant

Darren Sant was born in 1970 and raised in Stoke-on-Trent in Staffordshire which is in the United Kingdom. He moved to Hull in East Yorkshire in 2001.

After attending a few creative writing classes he started writing poetry. After moving to Hull he joined a writing group called the Renegade Writers who gained infamy by doing performance poetry with a Rock N Roll ethos. Following the split of the Renegade Writers he settled down a little and didn't write for a while.

Darren's stories have appeared in various online publications such as The Flash Fiction Offensive, Pulp Metal, Thrillers Killers N Chillers, The Killing Pandemic, Flash Jab Fiction and Shotgun Honey. Darren's creation The Longcroft Estate is the setting for a number of his stories. A collection of the first three of these tales was published by Byker Books in February 2012.

Gareth Spark

Gareth Spark was born in the middle of a blizzard on New Year's day, 1979. He grew up in Whitby, a small, ancient town on the North East coast of England and published his first book, a collection of poetry called At The Breakwater at age 22. He has since published two further collections (Ramraid and Rain in a dry land) as well as the crime thriller, Black Rain (Skrev Press, 2004). His short fiction has appeared in Out of the Gutter, Shotgun Honey, Near to the Knuckle, The Big Adios and Line Zero, among other journals and various anthologies. His story "American Tan" came 2nd in the GKBC International Short Story competition.

Martin Stanley

Martin Stanley was born in Middlesbrough in 1972. He was educated in Teesside and later in Bristol, where he studied graphic design.

He is the author of <u>The Gamblers</u>, a violent crime thriller set in Bristol, and <u>The Hunters</u>, the first in the Stanton brothers' series of crime thrillers. The brothers also appear in Martin's short story collection <u>The Greatest Show in Town</u>, and the novellas Bone Breakers, Green Eyed Monster, and The Curious Case of the Missing Moolah. The sequel to The Hunters, The Glasgow Grin, is due to appear later in 2014.

He lives, works and socialises in London.

You can find more stuff from Martin (such as short stories, reviews, and the occasional essay or comment) on www.thegamblersnovel.com and www.facebook.com/TheGamblersNovel

Mark Wilson

Mark Wilson is married father of two, born in Bellshill, Lanarkshire and currently living in Edinburgh with his wife, their son, Patrick and baby daughter, Cara.

Mark left Bellshill Academy in 1991, qualification-free. And worked his way through a huge number of jobs including, window-cleaner, delivery driver, Levi's salesman, microbiologist and cinema usher. Mark returned to full time education nine years later, earning his Highers and a degree in micro-biology before entering teaching.

Mark currently teaches Biology in a Fife secondary school and is founder of Paddy's Daddy Publishing, a company he set up to assist Scottish authors. He writes in his spare time, in lieu of sleep.

As well as the his autobiography, <u>Paddy's Daddy</u>, Mark is the author of five novels. <u>Bobby's Boy</u>, <u>Head Boy</u>, the bestselling <u>Naebody's Hero</u>, dEaDINBURGH, and The Man Who Sold His Son. His novels have been well received and feature Scottish characters.

Printed in Great Britain
by Amazon